D1484388

The Eridanos Library 20

Yury Tynyanov

Lieutenant Kijé
Young Vitushishnikov

Two novellas translated and introduced by
Mirra Ginsburg

Marsilio Publishers
New York

Original Russian titles *Podporuchik Kizhe*
and *Maloletny Vitushishnikov*

Copyright © 1990 Mirra Ginsburg

Originally published by Eridanos Press.

Of the present edition copyright ©1992
Marsilio Publishers, Corp.
853 Broadway
New York, New York 10003

ISBN 0-941419-77-0
LOC 88-80808

Contents

Introduction

by

Mirra Ginsburg

"If I had not had my childhood,
I would not understand history."

Yury Tynyanov—
Fragments toward an autobiography

"Documents often lie, like people . . .
I begin where the document ends."

Yury Tynyanov—
How We Write (1930)

Yury Tynyanov

Yury Tynyanov was a leading representative of the astonishing Russian cultural renaissance of the early decades of our century—that vast, miraculous emergence of genius in all the arts, which came to its most brilliant expression in the early post-revolutionary years and was so quickly and remorselessly extinguished by the end of the nineteen-twenties and early thirties.

Son of a Jewish doctor, Tynyanov was born in 1894 in Rezhitsa, in what is now the Latvian Republic, "some six hours' journey," he wrote in an autobiographical fragment, "from the birthplace of Mikhoels[*] and Chagall, and eight hours from the birthplace of Catherine I."

In Rezhitsa, he wrote, several peoples and several centuries lived side by side. Its population consisted chiefly of Russians, Byelorussians, Letts, Jews (worldly and Hassidic), a large number of Russian Old Believers, and an occasional infusion of visiting Gypsies. It was a typical small town with its share of madmen, eccentrics, drunks, and beggars. He de-

---

[*] Solomon Mikhoels, great Jewish actor, head of the State Jewish Theater founded in Petrograd in 1919.

scribes a madwoman who "marched along the street, driving her flock of children before her. Their number grew from year to year. Without benefit of Karamazov." He writes of Nikolay, in a green hunter's hat with a feather, who strode rapidly down the street and far out onto the highway promptly at the same time every day, so that housewives would shout to their neighbors, "Time to put up your soup—crazy Nikolay just went by." There were also savage fights among town rowdies, and battles between warring groups, such as the butchers and the organ-grinders, who belabored each other with long harness shafts.

Mystery plays still survived in his childhood: bakers and cobblers, dressed in paper caps and costumes, carrying lanterns and wooden swords, went from house to house, enacting the death of Artaxerxes.

But most colorful of all were the Old Believers who lived in their own community on the fringe of the town, faithful to the way of life and speech and worship they had preserved for centuries despite persecution by Church and Tsars. Tynyanov writes affectionately of their skilled artisans, their pride and loyalty in friendship, their wild weddings and divorces and remarriages, each marked by "archaic" drunkenness and furious rides on the horses they bred, cherished, adorned like women, and drove to the point of exhaustion. Tall men, in caftans and wide-brimmed hats, they came to the Lettish fairs (called by the old German word *Kermesse*) with their silent, stately wives dressed, for the holiday, in violet, green, blue, red, and yellow velvet coats. "The snow blazed with their colors." This was medieval Russia.

At the age of nine Tynyanov was sent to gymnasium in Pskov, one of the oldest Russian cities, its streets and buildings a living presence of the past. A walk outside the city limits led to terrifying roadside gallows. There were frequent hangings in the city, he writes, and wherever one went, prisons, and the clanking of chains from the courtyards behind the walls.

Tynyanov was growing up, steeped in Russian history.

Then, in 1912, on to the University of Petersburg, a vital center of brilliant scholarship, his chosen field philology and the history of Russian literature. It was a field that attracted many of the most original and gifted minds of the time, who became the founders of innovative schools and movements, enunciators of bold new theories and ideas. Tynyanov quickly became a part of this elite company. He was an early member of OPOYAZ, the Society for the Study of Poetic Language, and of the Formalist school of literary criticism, and found friendships that were to last a lifetime—with Boris Eichenbaum, Yulian Oxman, Victor Shklovsky.

The revolution opened new vistas and opportunities. Tynyanov's generation matured early. By the age of thirty he was already a famous and highly respected authority. From 1921 to 1930 he lectured on the history of Russian poetry of the 18th-20th centuries at the newly-founded Institute of History of the Arts in Petrograd, later Leningrad. Students, general listeners, and scholars flocked to his lectures, and recalled them decades later with admiration and gratitude.

In 1921 he published his first book, *Dostoyevsky and Gogol: Toward a Theory of Parody*, and, in 1924, *The Problem of Poetic Language*, his basic work in literary theory. In 1929 came his *Archaists and Innovators*, a collection of essays in literary history, theory, and criticism written during the preceding decade.

His other accomplishments in the course of that decade included several years as head of the scenario department of Sevzapkino (later Lenfilm). He wrote a number of scenarios based on stories by Gogol and Turgenev, as well as his own *Lieutenant Kijé*, (produced some time later with music by Prokofiev, who subsequently developed it into the "Lieutenant Kijé Suite"). He participated in the production of these and other films, and wrote film criticism and theoretical essays—fresh and original, as usual—on the art of film.

Three collections of his translations of Heine, a poet with whom he felt great affinity, appeared in the late 1920s and early 1930s. Throughout the 1930s, Tynyanov was also the editor of *The Poet's Library* series, founded by Gorky and entrusted to him. Fifty volumes of poetry appeared under his direction.

All of this, with unfailing warmth and gaiety, modestly, and with the lightest touch. And, especially in the last fifteen years of his life, with great courage, for he was stricken with multiple sclerosis in an increasingly severe form when he was barely thirty.

Tynyanov's turn to fiction was inevitable, given his temperament and his great talent. (Also, perhaps, given the rout of the innovative Formalist school and of OPOYAZ at the hands of the party critics and writers.) It began almost by chance. Korney Chukovsky, leading editor, critic, and children's writer, who attended Tynyanov's lecture on the early nineteenth century poet and critic Wilhelm Kyukhelbeker, asked him to write a short biography of the poet. Friend of Pushkin, quixotic idealist and participant in the Decembrist Uprising of 1825, Kyukhelbeker was sentenced to death, then reprieved by Nicholas I. He spent the rest of his life in solitary confinement in several fortress prisons and later in Siberian exile. Forgotten and unpublished for a hundred years, he was discovered and brought back to life by Tynyanov in the course of his studies of Pushkin and his circle. The short biography turned into a beautiful and tragic full-length novel, *Kyukhlia*, which won great and instant success on publication in 1925, and remains one of the classics of twentieth century Russian literature.

From then on fiction alternated with scholarly works. To the general, the abstraction of theory, Tynyanov added the specific, the search for the living reality of the past—a reality that turned out to be a mirror of the present.

In 1927 he wrote the satirical novella, *Lieutenant Kijé* (*Podporuchik Kizhe*, transformed in the present translation into *Lieutenant Nants*, for reasons that will be clear to the reader from the first pages of the novella), and completed the magnificent novel, the *Death of Vazir Mukhtar*, on the life and death, at the hands of a fanatical mob in Persia, of Alexander Griboyedov, diplomat, poet, author of the great comedy *Woe From Wit* (banned by the Tsar's censors), and one of the most complex and brilliant minds of his time.

These were followed by the novellas, *The Wax Figure*, on the death of Peter the Great and its aftermath, a dark and violent work and an extraordinary tour-de-force, written in 1930 in the language of Peter's time (and thus virtually untranslatable), and *Young Vitushishnikov*, in 1933.

In the 1930s, while working on one of his most ambitious projects, the novel based on the life of Pushkin, which was to complete the trilogy—Kyukhelbeker, Griboyedov, Pushkin—Tynyanov wrote in a draft of an introduction: "This book will not be a biography. The reader will not find in it exact facts, precise chronology, or a retelling of the findings of scholarly studies. That is not the task of a novelist, but the duty of a Pushkin scholar. In a novel, surmise often takes the place of a chronicle of events . . . What I want to do is to find *the truth of art* about the past, which is always the goal of the historical novelist."

In a fragment of autobiography, Tynyanov elaborates further his views on historical fiction:

"Literature differs from history, not by 'invention,' but by a greater, more intimate understanding of people and events, by deeper concern about them. . . . 'Invention' is a chance thing that depends not on the essence of the matter, but on the artist. It is when there is nothing of chance, only necessity, that the novel begins. But the look must be much deeper, the intuition and the daring much greater. And then comes the ultimate in art—the sense of discovered truth: this is how it could have been, this, perhaps, is how it was." (Alas, a dangerous approach, except in the hands of a great and scrupulous scholar and a very great writer.)

• •

Tynyanov was one of that rare breed—a great scholar, a brilliant and original thinker, and a great and profound artist, gifted, in addition, with immaculate taste and virtuosity, a marvelous sense of the absurd, and a rich capacity for both subtlety and laughter. A wellspring of wit and gaiety—and increasingly a man of profound pessimism and a tragic sense of history, which he shared with the best of his contemporaries—Blok, Akhmatova, Mandelstam, Zamyatin, Bulgakov, Platonov, Shvartz.

Whatever these writers of different backgrounds and different temperaments might have become in a quieter age, the violence and pressures of their time compelled an awareness and preoccupation common to all—an acute awareness of history, and preoccupation with the problem of power in society and the fate of the individual, and, especially, of the artist, and indeed of all culture, in the repressive state.

Tynyanov brought to this theme his profound knowledge of history, his unobstructed vision, vast talent, and absolute integrity—a quality that required enormous courage in those deeply troubled years.

His position, and his very survival in the Russia of his time, was paradoxical. He was not subjected to the overt massive persecution suffered by virtually all the great writers of the time, yet he was never quite forgiven for his early Formalist heresies, which he never recanted. As a "historical novelist," his position was also ambiguous. The great success of *Kyukhlia*, the approval and protection of Gorky (while still influential), kept him relatively out of reach of the zealots of Communist orthodoxy.

Nevertheless, he was repeatedly charged with the sins of "stylization," pessimism, and "deliberate escape into the past," instead of writing about the present—"the glorious achievements of socialist construction," in simple language accessible to all.

What his critics almost inexplicably—and fortunately for him—did not understand was that, in writing about the past, he *was* writing also about the present. That his work existed on two (and possibly more) time planes .

Almost all of Tynyanov's fiction is set in the late eighteenth and early nineteenth centuries. In his novels he speaks of genius martyred at the hands of Tsarism. His novellas are sharp satires on the Old Regime. This fitted in with the needs of the new rulers and their adherents, who failed, or refused, to see how literally they perpetuated the tragic pattern of Russian history.

And yet, the continuity of this pattern was inescapably clear: the palace revolutions; the violence within the ruling families (groups, factions, parties); the bloody throne; the oppression and terror, often random, in the palace and the land; the universal fear, among the rulers and the ruled; the all-pervasive system of spies, denunciations, and gendarmes; the universal servility; the brutal intolerance not only of dissent, but of any stirring of unofficial thought; the crushing of the individual, of art and the artist, who by his very nature must be free to deviate from the set and permitted. It was a pattern that persisted in Russia for centuries, and reasserted itself all too soon after the self-enthronement of the new masters—now with even greater ferocity and thoroughness, and unprecedented in scope.

The past, which was the object of his lifelong study, clearly served Tynyanov also as a metaphor, and his fiction was thus in the time-honored tradition of metaphoric writing, the refuge of many courageous spirits in dark times. In addition, the absolute specificity of historical facts, details, and events in his work may have served to fend off suspicion—or admission—that its thrust could *equally* have been aimed at the present. (Indeed, who would dare to say—this is about us.)

And, paradoxically again, it was perhaps his very illness that helped him to survive. It kept him largely out of the public eye and out of reach of the literary functionaries who were constantly pressing writers to attend meetings, travel to industrial sites and write enthusiastic reports, proclaim support of party policies, denounce colleagues, and demand their punishment for this or that "sin" against the party, the state, the people.

Nevertheless, danger remained, and fear remained, especially in the 1930s. Old friends disappeared, swept up in the waves of terror. The threat of a night visit, search, arrest, and all the possibilities that followed was ever present. Papers that might, however remotely, be incriminating, were burnt.

The novelist Veniamin Kaverin, Tynyanov's brother-in-law and dedicated friend, describes a visit to his home in late 1937. Tynyanov, he writes, took him to the window opening on the courtyard and said, "Look, do you see?"

He saw nothing but the usual view: the wall of the next building, the empty, narrow yard, an empty wooden shack on the patched roof of a barn—perhaps an abandoned pigeon-cote. "I don't see any-thing."

"Look closely."

And he saw. Not the yard, but the air in it, the dense, fine, almost invisible ash hanging motion-less in the narrow stone well.

"What is it?"

Tynyanov spoke bitterly, "They are burning mem-ory. It's been going on for a long time. Every night."

He grieved, Kaverin tells us, not only for the people who were being destroyed, but also for the loss of those unique, precious fragments that at-tested to their existence—photographs, letters, diaries —fragments of time, of life that added up to human history.

Yet even Tynyanov, ill and despairing, was com-pelled by the all-pervasive fear to join the epidemic of burning.

The novel based on Pushkin's life was never finished. Tynyanov had written numerous essays on Pushkin and his work. But the search for the *living* poet was evidently not easy. As though in awe be-fore the incandescent genius of his protagonist and the enormous responsibility of the task he was un-dertaking, he had approached it again and again, always putting it aside. He returned to it in earnest in the mid-1930s, when, for him, it was too late. Too ill, he had time enough to complete only the early parts, dealing with the poet's childhood and youth. He was no longer able to work at the library, and the materials he needed were brought to him by former students and friends. When the first volume, containing parts one and two, was published in 1937, the edition was immediately sold out—people fought to get the book.

In 1941, evacuated from besieged Leningrad, he stubbornly persisted with the work, dictating the final portion when he was no longer able to write. This part, the third, was published in a magazine, *Znamya*, in August, 1943. Four months later Tynyanov died, at the age of forty-nine, in a Moscow hospital.

Neither his fiction, nor his scholarly writings were reissued for many years after his death, as though he had fallen into total posthumous disfavor. It was not until 1956, during the so-called thaw, that his works began to reappear in print, including a three-volume edition of his fiction in 1959, and a collection of his essays, *Pushkin and His Contemporaries*, in 1969.

Thanks in large measure to the efforts of Kaverin, who was soon joined by a group of younger scholars and admirers, innumerable essays and papers on Tynyanov and his work have since appeared in journals and collections, among them several volumes of memoirs and warm tributes by fellow writers, scholars, filmmakers, former students and friends.

In Rezhitsa (now Resekne), his birthplace, a street has been named after him, and a museum has been established that bears his name. His writings, his theories and discoveries, far ahead of his time and still fresh and seminal, are widely studied today. Biennial conferences, so-called "Tynyanov Readings," are held in the town, where leading scholars and writers gather to discuss his legacy and allied problems of literature and linguistics. In the course of the 1980s, the proceedings of these conferences have been published in a series of volumes, which are treasured by scholars in the field.

His novels and novellas remain enormously popular. They are issued in editions of hundreds of thousands, and sell out within days of publication.

On the Novellas

While Tynyanov's novels, which examine Russian life and the destinies of three Russian poets of the early nineteenth century, are dark and powerful, the novellas offered in this volume may at first glance seem to be delightful, farcical excursions through the vanities and vagaries of a time long past. But behind the wit and the laughter, the darkness and violence—and the contemporary parallels—are also unmistakably present.

In the novels, his heroes are vastly unlike one another in temperament and gifts. Yet, free in spirit, their lives inescapably fall into the same pattern: they are destroyed by the massive hostile weight of the autocracy.

The novels speak in grief and anger. The novellas trip lightly. A supreme and subtle ironist, Tynyanov was able to treat dangerous ideas with ease and grace. This talent, too, was brought to the service of his reflections on the absurdity, the vanity and the inevitable cruelty of absolute power.

In the novellas there are no great poets—only Tsars and their servants; "the people," such as they are; and even "non-people." Here invention did not need to be curbed by respect for the protagonist and historical fact. And the historic characters themselves provided ample opportunity for the full play of Tynyanov's richly comic imagination.

With rare virtuosity, sensitivity, and tact, never laboring the point, he recreates the atmosphere, the flavor of a period by the very rhythms of his prose, the turn of phrase, the authenticity of verbal choices. And so with characters.

According to memoirs, Tynyanov was a superb actor who, effortlessly and almost instinctively, assumed the tone and image of people he spoke about, at times with affection, at times in caricature. This art of mimicry permeates his writing as well. In a sense, he writes from within his characters, just as he writes from within the historical time of his works.

The plot of *Lieutenant Kijé* (*Lieutenant Nants*) was based in part on incidents, perhaps apocryphal, recorded in a collection of anecdotes about the reign of Emperor Paul I[*]—the creation of a non-existent officer by a clerical error, and the demise of a living one "for the same reason." What Tynyanov did with these fragments is the fruit of his great comic genius. But he also went beyond the comic: he transformed anecdotes into metaphors, into the deeper truth of satire.

The world of Kijé is ruled by fear at all levels—above and below. It is a world that lives by orders, a world in which the words of orders are "very special words, unlike ordinary human speech." What they carry is "not simply meaning, but a life and power

---

[*] Paul I. *Collection of Anecdotes, Comments, Characteristics, Orders, etc.* Compiled by Alexander Geno and Tomich. St. Petersburg, 1901.

of their own." "An order somehow changes regiment, streets, people."

It is a topsy-turvy world where the nonexistent lives richly, and the alive, such as it is, such as it can be in that stifling society, is reduced to chaff, to dust that vanishes without a trace.

The tale that begins with hilarity turns into grotesque, into tragedy. Paul himself becomes not only a terrified madman vested with supreme power, but also a victim of this power and the terror it inevitably entails.

Lieutenant Kijé is one of the great tragi-comic parables of all time.

Young Vitushishnikov is another tale of the absurd. The action takes place during the reign of Nicholas I, who succeeded his brother, Alexander I—both of them Paul's sons. Nicholas is not a madman. He is merely a stiff, self-important, sentimental, meddling fool, obsessed with trifling details. Tynyanov's approach in this novella is quite different. The number of characters is greater, the action wider in scope, and Tynyanov treats us to a brilliant satire of another kind.

Bringing his mimic art into play, he mocks the smug, pompous rhythms and vocabulary of the Emperor, the thought and speech of his courtiers, the meanness, abject fear and subservience of officials, from ministers to the lowly policeman—and the future policeman, young Vitushishnikov. He mocks the events as they take place, the "historical documents" supposedly recording them, the testimony of "witnesses," and the diligent historians who place their trust in them. And all of it with tongue in cheek, with consummate restraint, intelligence and taste.

He plays with style, impaling his characters on their own words—as in the Emperor's ruminations, the policeman's report, the boy's account of his role in that great event of state—the Emperor's visit to a tavern in search of two thirsty soldiers, and Bulgarin's version of the "historic event." The scene in which this version is created is a small masterpiece in itself.

Tynyanov's characterizations are deft and brief, often achieved by an oblique, ironic thrust. Thus Bulgarin, slavish upholder of the autocracy, traitor, flunkey and police informer, commenting on Pushkin soon after his death—"An empty vessel," and "There was not much difference between us. We both had always tried to please our superiors." This, about Russia's greatest poet and one of the freest spirits of his time.

Young Vitushishnikov is high comedy, many-faceted, marvelously inventive, and, in the end, again a bitter commentary on the stultifying weight of autocratic rule.

A Note on the Translation

Among twentieth century Russian writers, Tynyanov is one of the most resistant to translation. He
writes with the compressed brevity of poetry and,
like poetry, his prose often presents insuperable
barriers.

Russian permits highly charged brevities. So does
English. But their brevities do not coincide. Tynyanov's style, especially in the novellas, is oblique, al-
lusive, and incredibly laconic. Because of this, and
of his enormously witty use of language, the individual word becomes crucially important. A
single word may resonate with a wealth of associa-
tions. The "equivalent" word in English—as "right"
as can be possible in two unrelated languages—will
often be dead wrong. In Tynyanov's work there are
many seemingly ordinary words that turn out to be
utterly intractable in *his* context, and the translator
must tread a tenuous line to approximate the original. The resonances of the two languages do not
coincide, and sometimes do not even overlap.

Tynyanov's artful prose transports the Russian
reader to the period of the work and defines his

characters, even as they speak or think. This, too, must suffer in translation. Time and experience do not coincide.

And yet, and yet . . . you challenge the difficulties, and seek, despite them, to capture the *life* of the prose, the author's voice, temper, wit, the music and the magic of the work.

In addition, because Tynyanov's writing is so concrete in detail and reference, often almost a kind of shorthand that is instantly meaningful to the literate Russian reader, I have provided for each novella a Cast of Characters, the Scene of Action, and a small number of Notes to sketch in some of the background against which the novellas are set, and so to open a wider perspective to English-speaking readers.

In conclusion, I wish to thank my friends Pat Kolb and Mary Mackler, who read parts of the manuscript and offered much-needed encouragement and valuable comments, and Eugene Beshenkovsky, for his help with linguistic and historical problems. I am warmly grateful, also, to a far-away friend, Elena Chukovskaya, for her generous help in my search for biographical material on Tynyanov. And finally, thanks to Juan García de Oteyza, publisher of Eridanos Press, for bringing Tynyanov to life in English.

Lieutenant Kijé

Cast of Characters

Historical:

Emperor Paul I (Paul Petrovich), born in 1754. Reigned 1796 - 1801. Mentally unbalanced at the time of his accession to the throne and throughout his reign. Military martinet who introduced Prussian precision and discipline into the life of the army and court. Given to mad fits of rage. Haunted by the memory of the recent French Revolution. Obsessed by hatred of his mother, Catherine II, who conspired in the deposition and, possibly, murder of his presumed father, Peter III, also mad, in 1762, upon which she had herself crowned Empress of Russia, delaying Paul's accession by thirty-four years.

Assassinated in a palace revolution in his "impregnable" St. Petersburg castle, after a five-year rule of arbitrary terror and measures aimed chiefly at reversing Catherine's policies and eradicating the memory of her favorite, Potemkin.

Arakcheyev, Alexey Andreyevich (1769 - 1834). One of the most influential men at the court of

Emperor Paul I. Appointed Commandant of St. Petersburg in 1796, raised to the rank of Major-General a day later, given the title of Baron in 1797, and that of Count in 1798. Extreme reactionary.

Nelidova. Maid-in-Waiting at the court and the Emperor's favorite, whose fortune is on the wane.

Neledinsky-Meletsky, Yury Alexandrovich (1752 - 1828). Civilian, minor poet, held important posts at court, including that of Secretary of State.

Count von Pahlen, Pyotr Alexeyevich (1745 - 1826). Military Governor of St. Petersburg, the Emperor's most trusted adviser toward the end of his reign, and leader in the conspiracy to depose and assassinate him.

Bennigsen, Leonty Leontievich (1743 - 1826). General, later participated in the war of 1812.

Fictional:

Courier, who appears in the Emperor's dream.

The Emperor's Aide-de-Camp.

Army clerk, young and inexperienced.

Lieutenant Nants, born of a clerical error. (Kijé in Russian.)

Lieutenant Sinukhayev, killed by a clerical error.

Commander of the Preobrazhensky Regiment (the traditional Court Guard since Peter the Great).

Young soldier.

Old soldier.

Auditor of the Senate Military School.

Surgeon Sinukhayev, the Lieutenant's father, in the service of Baron Arakcheyev.

Maid-in-Waiting to Nelidova, later wife of Lieutenant Nants and mother of his child.

Amorous officer.

Courtiers, soldiers, commanders of outposts, peasants, merchants, street vendors and street urchins.

Scene:

Russia, at the end of the XVIIIth Century.

The Imperial Court and Palace at Pavlovskoye.

Gatchina, royal residence on the outskirts of St. Petersburg, where Paul spent most of the years of his mother's reign, barred from participation in public affairs and surrounded by a small court of his own, strictly disciplined along military lines.

St. Petersburg, then less than a hundred years old.

The Emperor's "impregnable" castle in St. Petersburg, where he was subsequently assassinated.

1.

The Emperor Paul dozed at an open window. Silence reigned in the Imperial Palace in Pavlovskoye. Disturbances were forbidden in that after-dinner hour when the food slowly grapples with the body. Paul Petrovich reclined in his high armchair, protected from behind and from the sides by a glass screen. He was dreaming his usual after-dinner dream:

> He was sitting in the trimmed little garden of his palace in Gatchina, and the plump cupid in the corner stared at him as he dined with his family. Then a creaking was heard in the distance, bouncing monotonously over the ruts and hollows of the road. Paul Petrovich discerned a three-cornered hat, galloping horses, a cabriolet, dust. He hid under the table, for the three- cornered hat was a courier, coming for him from St. Petersburg.

"*Nous sommes perdus* . . . We're lost . . . " he shouted hoarsely to his wife from under the table, so that she, too, would hide.

Under the table there was not enough air, and the creaking was now there, the cabriolet was pressing in upon him with its shafts.

The courier looked under the table, found Paul Petrovich, and reported:

"Your Majesty! Her Majesty your mother is dead."

But when Paul Petrovich began to climb out from under the table, the courier filliped him on the forehead and cried out:

"Help!"

Paul Petrovich brushed him away . . . and caught a fly.

And so he sat there, goggling his gray eyes at the window of his palace, suffocating with food and anguish, listening, the buzzing fly in his hand.

Someone was shouting "Help!" under the window.

2.

The old army clerk of the office of the Preobrazhensky Regiment had been deported to Siberia.

The new clerk, very young, still no more than a boy, sat at the table, writing. His hand trembled because he was late.

He was to finish transcribing the regimental order exactly by six o'clock in the morning, so that the Adjutant on duty could take it to the palace, where the Aide-de-Camp to His Majesty, adding the order to others of a similar nature, would present them to the Emperor at nine. Lateness was a major offense. The clerk had risen earlier than usual, but he had spoiled the first copy, and was writing another one. In the first copy he made two mistakes: he entered Lieutenant Sinukhayev as dead, since Sinukhayev's name followed that of the newly deceased Major Sokolov. He also made the following absurd entry: instead of "and the Second Lieutenants Steven, Rybin, and Azancheyev are appointed," he wrote "and the Second Lieuten. Nants, Steven, Rybin, and Azancheyev are appointed." An officer had come in while he was writing the word "Lieutenants," and he sprang up to salute him, leaving off at the "n." Then he returned to his work and, in confusion, wrote "Lieuten. Nants."

He knew that if the order was not ready by six, the Adjutant would shout "Take him! Under arrest!" And he would be taken. Therefore his hand refused to work. He wrote more and more slowly, and suddenly squirted a large, beautiful, fountain-like blot on the order.

Only ten minutes remained.

Leaning back, the clerk looked at the clock as if it were a living person. Then his fingers, which seemed detached from his body and moving of their own volition, began to fumble among the papers for a clean sheet, although there were none on the table and he knew perfectly well that they were in the cupboard, stacked away in a neat pile.

However, as he searched in sheer desperation, simply for form's sake, he was struck anew.

Another document, equally important, was also incorrect.

According to the Emperor's Order No. 940, prohibiting the use of certain words in reports, the word *inspect* was to be used in place of "review," *fulfill* instead of "execute," and *guard* instead of "watch." Furthermore, "detail" was not to be used under any circumstances; instead, the word to be used was *detachment*.

In the case of civil statutes, it was further stated that the word *class* should be used instead of "grade," *assembly* instead of "society," and *merchant* or *burgher* instead of "citizen."

This, however, was written in small letters at the bottom of Order No. 940, which hung on the wall right before the clerk's eyes, and he had not read it. As for *inspect,* etc., he had learned it all by heart on the very first day and remembered it well.

Yet in the paper prepared for the signature of the Commander of the Regiment and addressed to Baron Arakcheyev, it was written:

"Having *reviewed,* upon the recommendation of Your Excellency, the *details* of the *watch* assigned to duty in St. Petersburg and the vicinity, I have the honor of reporting that the above has been *executed. . . .* "

But that was not all.

The first line of the report, which he himself had copied, was:

"Your Excellency, Dear Sir."

Now, every child knew that a salutation written in a single line meant a command, but in the reports of a subordinate, especially to such a personage as Baron Arakcheyev, the only permissible form was two lines:

"Your Excellency,
  Dear Sir"

which indicated proper subordination and courtesy.

And if he could merely be held accountable for failing to notice and pay timely attention to "having reviewed," etc., the "Dear Sir" was entirely his own mistake.

Utterly dazed and no longer aware of what he was doing, the clerk began to correct the second paper. Copying it, he instantly forgot the order, which was much more urgent.

So that when the Aide-de-Camp sent for the order, the clerk looked at the clock, then at the messenger, and suddenly handed him the page with the dead Lieutenant Sinukhayev.

Then he sat down and, still trembling, wrote:
Excellencies, detachments, guard . . .

3.

Exactly at nine the Emperor pulled the cord, and the bell rang in the palace. His Majesty's Aide-de-Camp entered with the daily report. Paul Petrovich sat in the same position as yesterday, at the window, behind the glass screen.

But now he neither slept nor dozed, and the expression on his face was different.

Like everyone else in the palace, the Aide-de-Camp knew that the Emperor was angry. But he also knew that anger seeks further exasperations, and the more it finds, the more it rages. Therefore, the report could under no circumstances be omitted.

He stood at attention before the glass screen and the Emperor's back, and began to read the report.

Paul Petrovich did not turn to the Aide-de-Camp. His breathing was slow and heavy. All day yesterday they had been unable to discover who it was that shouted "Help!" under his window, and at night the Emperor woke twice in anguish.

"Help!" was an absurd cry, and at first Paul Petrovich was not very angry. He simply reacted like any other man who has had a bad dream and was prevented from seeing it to the end. For the dream might have had a happy ending, and then it would still augur well. Later he became curious: who could have shouted "Help!" under his very window, and why? But when it turned out to be impossible to find the culprit in his entire frightened palace, his anger became great. The affair turned thus: in his own palace, after dinner, a man was able to cause a disturbance and remain undiscovered. Besides, there was no telling what had prompted such a cry. Perhaps it was the warning of a repentant plotter. Or, perhaps, a man was gagged and strangled in those shrubs, which were already searched three times to no avail. He seemed to have vanished from the earth. They should . . . But what should they—if the man was not found?

The guard should be doubled. Everywhere.

Paul Petrovich stared without turning at the square green shrubs, so much like those in the Trianon. They were neatly trimmed. And yet it was not known who had been among them.

And, without looking at the Aide-de-Camp, he flung back his right arm. The Aide-de-Camp knew what that meant: in times of wrath the Emperor never turned. The Aide-de-Camp deftly slipped the order to the Preobrazhensky Guards Regiment into the outstretched hand, and Paul Petrovich carefully began to read it. Then the hand was flung back again, and the Aide-de-Camp quickly and silently picked up a pen from the desk, dipped it into the inkwell, shook it, and lightly placed it in the waiting hand, smearing himself with ink. All this was performed in an instant. Soon the signed sheet flew back. In that manner the Aide-de-Camp handed the Emperor all the sheets, and, signed or merely read, they flew back at him one after the other. He was beginning to grow accustomed to it, and to hope that all would yet be well, when the Emperor jumped off his elevated seat.

With little steps he ran up to the Aide-de-Camp. His face was red and his eyes dark.

He approached the Aide face to face and sniffed at him. The Emperor did this whenever he was suspicious. Then he seized the Aide-de-Camp by the sleeve with two fingers and pinched him.

The Aide-de-Camp stood at attention, holding the sheets in his hand.

"You don't know your duty, sir," said Paul Petrovich hoarsely. "Coming up from behind!"

He pinched the Aide again.

"I'll knock the Potemkin spirit out of you.[1] Get out!"

And the Aide-de-Camp backed out through the door, closing it silently.

As soon as he was alone, Paul Petrovich quickly unwound the scarf around his neck and slowly began to rip the shirt on his chest. His mouth twisted and his lips trembled.

The *great wrath* was beginning.

4.

The order to the Preobrazhensky Regiment, signed by the Emperor, was angrily corrected by him. The words "And the Second Lieuten. Nants, Steven, Rybin, and Azancheyev are appointed" drew his displeasure. He wrote a huge "R" after the "Lieuten." and crossed out several letters. Then he wrote over them, "Second Lieutenant Nants assigned to guard duty." The rest met with no objections.

The order was transmitted.

When the Commander of the regiment received it, he strained his memory for a long time, trying to recall the lieutenant with the strange name, Nants. He consulted the roster of all the officers of the Preobrazhensky Regiment, but found no officer of that name. Neither was the name to be found in the lists of the common soldiers. It was incomprehensible. The clerk was probably the only person in the world who knew what it was all about, but no one asked him, and he told no one. However, the Emperor's order had to be carried out. And yet it could not be carried out because Second Lieutenant Nants was not to be found anywhere in the regiment.

The Commander thought of consulting Baron Arakcheyev, but immediately abandoned the idea. Baron Arakcheyev lived in Gatchina, and the outcome was doubtful anyway.

And, since one always turns to kin when in trouble, the Commander quickly accounted himself related to His Majesty's Aide-de-Camp, Sablukov, and galloped off to Pavlovskoye.

Pavlovskoye was in an uproar, and at first the Aide-de-Camp refused to admit the Commander.

Then he listened with a squeamish mien, and was just about to send him to the devil—he had troubles enough on his hands—when suddenly he frowned, flashed a glance at the Commander, and all at once the glance was transformed: it became inspired.

The Aide-de-Camp said slowly:

"The matter is not to be reported to the Emperor. Consider that Second Lieutenant Nants exists, and assign him to guard duty."

Without a second look at the distraught Commander, he turned, drew himself up to his full height, and stalked away, leaving the dazed man to his fate.

5.

Lieutenant Sinukhayev was a seedy sort of a lieutenant. His father was surgeon to Baron Arakcheyev, and the Baron quietly slipped the surgeon's son into the regiment—in reward for the pills that had restored his health. The son's honest and dull-witted face pleased the Baron. In the regiment, the Lieutenant was not on intimate footing with any-one, but neither did he shun his comrades. He talked little, was fond of tobacco, did not run after wom-en, and—scarcely a fitting diversion for a gallant officer—took pleasure in playing the oboe d'amore.

His ammunition was always spotless.

When the regimental order was being read, Sinu-khayev stood stiffly upright, and his mind, as usual, was innocent of thought.

Suddenly he heard his name and pricked up his ears, like a dozing horse at the sudden crack of the whip.

"Lieutenant Sinukhayev, dead of fever, is to be considered separated from the service."

At that moment the Commander, who was read-ing the order, involuntarily glanced at the spot where Sinukhayev usually stood, and his hand, with the paper in it, dropped.

Sinukhayev was in his customary place. Presently, however, the Commander resumed his reading—though not quite as distinctly as before. He read about Steven, Azancheyev, and Nants, and so on to the end. Maneuvers began and Sinukhayev should have moved with the rest in figure exercises. In-stead, he remained standing.

He was accustomed to regarding the words of orders as very special words, unlike ordinary human speech. What they carried was not simply meaning, but a life and power of their own. The question was not whether or not an order was obeyed. Even if it was not obeyed, an order somehow changed regiments, streets, people.

When he heard the Commander's words, he remained fixed to the spot like a man who did not trust his ears. He strained after the words. And then he ceased to doubt. The order had unquestionably referred to him. And when his column moved, he was no longer certain that he was alive.

From the sensation in his hand, which rested on the hilt of his sword, from the slight constriction caused by the tight belt, the heaviness of his pigtail, which had been freshly greased that very morning, it might be inferred that he was alive, but at the same time he knew that something was amiss, something was irreparably spoiled. The possibility of an error in the order never entered his mind. On the contrary, it seemed to him that he was alive through some oversight, some blunder on his own part. Through negligence he had failed to notice something and duly report it.

In any case, he was spoiling all the figures in the parade, standing on the square like a signpost, without thought of stirring.

As soon as the parade was over, the Commander flew at the Lieutenant. He was red. It was truly fortunate that the Emperor, who was resting at Pavlovskoye, had stayed away because of the heat. The Commander wanted to bellow: "To the guardhouse!" But he needed a more resonant sound to give full vent to his rage and was about to roar, rolling his "r"s: "Under ar-rest!"—when suddenly his jaws snapped, as if he had accidentally caught a fly in his mouth. And thus he stood before Lieutenant Sinukhayev for two or three minutes.

Then, recoiling as from the plague, he turned and strode away.

He remembered that Lieutenant Sinukhayev was separated from the service by reason of death, and restrained himself because he did not know how to speak to such a man.

6.

Paul Petrovich paced his room, stopping from time to time.

He was listening.

Since the day when, clad in dusty boots and a traveling cloak, the Emperor had thundered with his spurs out of the chamber where his mother was still gasping her last breath, and slammed the door upon her, it had been observed of the royal temper that wrath usually turned into great wrath, and great wrath ended, after two or three days, in fear or in melting sentiment.

The chimeras on the stairways in Pavlovskoye were done by the wild Brenna, and the walls and ceilings by Cameron[2], lover of tender hues that swooned and languished in the sight of all. On the one hand— the open maws of rearing, half-human lions, and on the other—the most exquisite sensibility.

In addition, two lanterns hung from the ceiling in the palace hall, a gift from the recently beheaded Louis XVI. Paul had received this gift in France, when traveling abroad under the name of Count Northern.

The lanterns were of high workmanship, with walls that softened the light.

But Paul Petrovich avoided lighting them.

There was also the clock, a gift from Marie Antoinette, which stood on the jasper table. The hour hand was a golden Saturn with a long scythe, and the minute hand—a Cupid with an arrow.

When the clock struck noon or midnight, Saturn's scythe covered the Cupid's arrow. This signified that time conquers love.

However, the clock was never wound up.

And so, there was Brenna in the garden, Cameron on the walls, and overhead—in the emptiness beneath the ceiling—swayed the lanterns of Louis XVI.

In times of great wrath, Paul Petrovich assumed a certain likeness to one of Brenna's lions.

On such days, rods hailed, as from a clear sky, over entire regiments; in the dark of the night, by the flare of torchlights, heads were chopped on the Don; hapless soldiers, clerks, lieutenants, generals, and governors general marched on foot to Siberia.

The usurper of the throne, his mother, was dead. He knocked out the Potemkin spirit from court and land as once Ivan the Fourth[3] had knocked out the Boyar spirit. He scattered Potemkin's bones upon the wind and leveled his grave. He eradicated every vestige of his mother's taste. The taste of a usurper! Gold, rooms spread with Indian silks, rooms filled with Chinese porcelain, with Dutch tile stoves, and the room of blue glass—a snuff-box. A circus! The Roman and Greek medals she had been so proud of! He ordered them melted down to gild his castle.

And yet the spirit, the scent, the tang of her remained.

He smelled it all around him. Perhaps that was why Paul Petrovich was in the habit of sniffing people.

And overhead, the French gallows-corpse, the lantern, swayed and swayed.

And the fear was rising. The Emperor felt that there was not enough air. He was not afraid of his wife, nor of his older sons, any of whom, remembering the example of their jolly mother-in-law and grandmother, might stab him to death with a fork and mount the throne.

He was not afraid of the suspiciously cheerful ministers or the suspiciously gloomy generals. Neither did he fear anyone among the fifty-million-headed rabble which squatted on the hillocks, swamps, sands, and fields of his Empire and which he never was able to envisage. He feared none of these by themselves. But together they were a sea, and he was drowning in it.

And he sent out orders to fortify his St. Petersburg castle with moats and outposts, to raise the drawbridge on its chains. But even the chains were uncertain—they were guarded by sentries.

And when the great wrath was turning to great fear, the Office of Criminal Affairs worked feverishly, and someone was hung up by the hands, and the floor collapsed under someone, while torturers awaited him below.

Therefore, when the steps heard from the Emperor's chamber were now short, now long, now suddenly stumbling, people looked at one another in silent anguish, and few smiled.

The chamber was filled with great fear.

The Emperor walked in it.

7.

Lieutenant Sinukhayev stood on the very same spot where he had been when the Commander swooped down to reprimand him and suddenly stopped short and walked away.

There was no one around.

After drill, Lieutenant Sinukhayev usually took a deep breath and relaxed his military bearing; his arms turned limp and he walked at ease back to the barracks. All his limbs would swing loosely, as though he were a civilian.

At home, in the officers' barracks, the Lieutenant would unbutton his coat and settle down to play his oboe d'amore. Then he would fill his pipe and stare out of the window, at the large tract of wasteland that had once been a garden. The trees had been chopped down and the barren tract was now called Tsaritsa's Meadow. In the meadow there was no variety, no greenery of any kind, nothing but the tracks of horses and soldiers in the sand.

The Lieutenant liked everything about smoking: filling the pipe, tamping down the tobacco, inhaling and blowing out the smoke. A man who smokes is a solid man; he will never be lost. These activities were quite enough for him, because soon it was evening, and he would go out to visit an acquaintance or simply to take a stroll.

He enjoyed the politeness of the simple folk. Once, when he sneezed, a townsman quipped pleasantly: "A finger in the nose smells as good as a rose."

Before going to sleep he would play a game of cards with his orderly. He had taught the man a few simple games. When the orderly lost, the Lieutenant would slap him on the nose with the deck; when the Lieutenant lost, he did not slap the orderly. Before retiring, he inspected the ammunition polished by his orderly, then he curled, braided and greased his own pigtail, and went to bed.

On this day, however, he did not relax as usual after drill. His muscles seemed knotted, and no breath could be heard escaping the Lieutenant's tightly shut lips. He looked around at the parade grounds and they were unfamiliar to him. At any rate, he had never before noticed the cornices over the windows of the red official building, or its muddy window panes.

The round cobblestones were as unlike each other as different brothers.

The military city of St. Petersburg lay before him in strict order, in gray regularity, with its barren tracts, its rivers and the bleary eyes of its pavement— an altogether unfamiliar city.

And then he understood that he was indeed dead.

8.

Paul Petrovich heard the steps of his Aide-de-Camp. Like a cat he stole up to the armchair behind the glass screen and sat down as firmly as though he had been sitting all the time.

He knew the steps of his courtiers. Sitting with his back to them, he recognized the easy stride of the confident, the hopping tread of flatterers, and the light, airy steps of the frightened. He never heard straight, honest steps.

This time the Aide-de-Camp walked confidently, with a slight shuffle. Paul Petrovich half turned his head.

The Aide came to the center of the screen and bowed his head.

"Your Majesty, it was Second Lieutenant Nants who shouted 'Help!'"

"Who's he?"

The fear was easing; it had found a name.

But the Aide-de-Camp had not expected the question, and he stepped lightly back.

"He is the Lieutenant who was appointed to guard duty, Your Majesty."

"And why did he shout it?" The Emperor stamped his foot. "I am listening, sir."

The Aide-de-Camp was silent for a moment.

"Just out of foolishness," he replied.

"Order an inquest. Have him flogged, and on foot to Siberia."

9.

And so began the life of Second Lieutenant Nants.

When the clerk had copied the order, Second Lieutenant Nants was an error, a clerical slip, nothing more. It might have gone unnoticed and would have drowned in a sea of papers. And, since the order was in no way remarkable, later historians would not even have troubled to reproduce it.

The captious eye of Paul Petrovich extracted it, and with a firm hand invested it with dubious life: the error became a Lieutenant—without a face, but with a name.

Later, the Aide-de-Camp's quick inspiration sketched in his face as well, though faintly, as in a dream. It was he who had shouted "Help!" under the palace window.

And now this face solidified and took shape: Second Lieutenant Nants turned out to be a malefactor, who was to be sentenced to the rack or, at best, the whipping post, and then to penal exile in Siberia.

This was reality.

Until now he had been merely the anxiety of the clerk, the perplexity of the Commander, and the saving inspiration of the Aide-de-Camp.

From now on, though, the whipping post, the lashes, and the trek to Siberia were his own personal affair.

The order had to be carried out. Second Lieutenant Nants had to be separated from the military, turned over to the judicial authorities, and then marched off along the green-bordered road straight to Siberia.

And all this was done.

The Commander, facing his regiment in full formation, called out the name of Second Lieutenant Nants in the thunderous voice of a man in utter dismay.

A whipping post was ready nearby, and two guardsmen tightened leather straps around it, at the head and the foot. Two guardsmen, standing on either side of it, brought down their cats-o'-nine-tails on the smooth wood. A third man counted. And the regiment looked on.

Since the wood had been polished to a high gloss by thousands of bellies, the whipping post did not seem altogether vacant. Though no one was on it, it seemed as though someone was there all the same. The soldiers frowned as they watched the silent whipping post, and by the end of the execution the Commander turned crimson, as he always did, and his nostrils flared.

Then the straps were loosened, and it seemed as though someone's shoulders had been freed. Two guardsmen approached and waited for the command.

They marched off down the street, away from the regiment, with even steps, their guns on their shoulders, and from time to time they glanced out of the corners of their eyes, not at each other, but at the space between them.

A young soldier, just recently recruited, stood in the ranks. He watched the execution with interest. He thought that everything he saw was quite the usual thing and that it happened frequently in military service.

In the evening, though, he began to fidget on his cot and asked the old soldier lying in the next cot:

"Say, Uncle, who is our Emperor?"

"Paul Petrovich, stupid," the old man answered in a frightened voice.

"And did you ever see him?"

"I did," the old man snapped. "And so will you."

They were silent. But the old soldier could not fall asleep. He kept twisting and turning. Ten minutes passed.

"Why do you ask?" the old man suddenly asked the boy.

"Who knows," the young man answered willingly. "They talk and talk—the Emperor! But who knows who he is? Maybe it's nothing but talk. . . . "

"Stupid," the old man said, glancing uneasily around him. "You'd better keep your mouth shut, you country bumpkin."

Another ten minutes went by. The barracks were dark and silent.

"He's there all right," the old man whispered into the young man's ear, "only he's not the real one—they've slipped in someone else."

10.

Lieutenant Sinukhayev attentively examined the room where he had lived until that day.

The room was spacious, with a low ceiling. On the wall there was a portrait of a man in his middle years, with eyeglasses and a small pigtail. This was the Lieutenant's father, the surgeon Sinukhayev.

The surgeon lived in Gatchina. But as he stared at the portrait, the Lieutenant was no longer certain of it. Maybe he lived there, and maybe he didn't.

Then he looked at Lieutenant Sinukhayev's belongings: the oboe d'amore in its wooden case, the curling iron, the jar with powder, the sand dish. And all those things looked back at him. He turned his eyes away.

And so he stood there in the middle of the room, waiting for something. He couldn't have been waiting for his orderly. And yet it was precisely his orderly who cautiously stepped into the room and halted in front of the Lieutenant. He opened his mouth a little and stood before the Lieutenant, staring at him.

He probably stood like that always, awaiting orders, but the Lieutenant looked at him as though seeing him for the first time, and dropped his eyes.

Death had to be concealed for a while, like a crime. In the evening a young man entered his room, sat down at the table on which lay the case with the oboe d'amore, took it out of the case, blew into it and, obtaining no sound, put it away in the corner.

Then he called the orderly and told him to bring some wine. He never once glanced at Lieutenant Sinukhayev.

The Lieutenant asked in a constricted voice:

"Who are you?"

The young man, who was sipping the wine, answered with a yawn: "Auditor of the Senate Military

School." And he told the orderly to make the bed. Then he began to undress, and Lieutenant Sinukhayev watched him for a long time, nimbly pulling off his boots and dropping them with a thud, unbuttoning his clothes, covering himself with the blanket, and yawning. At last, stretching, the young man looked up at Lieutenant Sinukhayev's arm, and suddenly pulled out the linen handkerchief tucked into the cuff of the Lieutenant's sleeve. He blew his nose, and yawned once more.

At this point, Lieutenant Sinkhayev finally re gained his voice and protested limply that this was against regulations.

The Auditor replied indifferently that, on the contrary, everything was strictly according to regulations. He was acting in accord with Paragraph No. 2, in view of the former Sinukhayev's recent demise. Moreover, he suggested that the Lieutenant take off his uniform, which, in his judgment, was still quite presentable, and put on a uniform no longer fit for wear.

Lieutenant Sinukhayev began to remove his uniform and the Auditor helped him, explaining that the late Sinukhayev might not do it properly himself.

Afterwards the former Sinukhayev put on a uniform no longer fit for wear, and stood a while, afraid that the Auditor might take away his gloves. He had long yellow gloves with square fingers—a part of the regulation outfit. He had heard once that losing one's gloves foretokened dishonor. A lieutenant who wore gloves was still a lieutenant, whatever else he might lack. Therefore, pulling on his gloves, the former Sinukhayev turned and walked away.

All night he wandered along the streets of St. Petersburg without even trying to direct his steps anywhere. Toward morning he felt tired and sat down on the ground near some building. He dozed off for a few minutes. Then he suddenly jumped up and strode away without looking to either side.

Soon he crossed the city limits. The sleepy clerk at the city gates absently wrote down his name.

He never returned to the barracks.

11.

The Aide-de-Camp was a wily man, and he told no one about Lieutenant Nants and his stroke of luck. Like everybody else, he had enemies. Therefore he merely told some people here and there that the man who had shouted "Help!" was found.

But this produced a strange effect in the women's quarters of the palace.

Two wings had been added to the front of the palace built by Cameron, topped by columns that were as slender as fingers striking a clavecin. These two wings were rounded like a cat's paws when the cat plays with a mouse. One of those wings was occupied by the Maid-in-Waiting Nelidova with her retinue.

Very often Paul Petrovich, guiltily slinking past the guards, made his way to this wing. And once the guards had seen the Emperor bolt out with his wig askew, a lady's slipper flying after him.

Although Nelidova was only a Maid-in-Waiting, she had her own Maids-in-Waiting as well.

And now, when the news reached the women's wing that the man who had cried "Help!" had been found, one of Nelidova's Maids-in-Waiting fell into a brief faint.

Like Nelidova, she was curly-haired and slender as a shepherd boy.

During the reign of grandmother Elizabeth,[4] the Maids-in-Waiting were encased in stiffly clattering brocades and rustling silks, and frightened nipples would suddenly peep out of them. Such was the fashion.

Then came amazons fond of masculine attire, with long velvet tails and stars at the nipples. They vanished with the usurper of the throne.

Now women had turned into curly-headed shepherd boys.

And so, one of them dropped into a brief faint.

Raised from the floor by her mistress and wakening from unconsciousness, she told her about the tryst she was to have had with an officer at that fateful hour. She had, however, been unable to absent herself from the upper story. Glancing out of the window she saw the enamored officer, forgetful of all caution and perhaps unaware that he was standing under the Emperor's own window, making signs to her from below.

She waved her hand at him and opened her eyes wide to indicate horror. Her lover, however, thought that he had become an object of disgust to her and cried out piteously, "Help!"

Without losing her head, she quickly flattened her nose with her finger and pointed down. At this pug-nosed gesture, the officer was aghast and vanished instantly.

She never saw him again, and since the entire amorous adventure had been so brief, she did not even know his name.

Now he had been discovered and exiled to Siberia. Nelidova began to think.

Her own star was waning, and although she would not admit it to herself, the time for flying slippers was long past.

Her relations with the Aide-de-Camp were frigid, and she was reluctant to appeal to him. The Emperor's condition was doubtful. In such cases she was now in the habit of turning to a certain civilian but powerful personage, Yury Alexandrovich Neledinsky-Meletsky.

And so she did on this occasion, sending him a note with her valet.

The brawny valet, who had carried such notes before, was always astonished at the puny size of the powerful man. Meletsky was a singer and a Secretary of State. He sang "Swift Waters" and had a sweet tooth for shepherdesses. His stature was of the smallest, his mouth was honeyed, but his eyebrows were shaggy. Besides, he was a sly fox. Looking up at the broad-shouldered valet, he said:

"Tell them not to worry. Let them wait. All this will be resolved."

However, he was himself somewhat fearful, quite unsure of how it would be resolved. And so when one of his young shepherdesses, formerly called Avdotya but now known as Selimene, opened his door, he fiercely raised his eyebrow at her.

Yury Alexandrovich's house servants were mostly young shepherdesses.

12.

The guards walked and walked.

From tollgate to tollgate, from outpost to fortress, they marched forward, glancing worriedly now and then at the important space marching between them.

This was not the first time they convoyed an exile to Siberia, but they had never before been placed in charge of such a criminal. When they had first come out of the city limits, they had some doubts. They heard no clanking chains and did not have to urge the prisoner on with their rifle butts. But later they decided that this was none of their business; it was the state's affair, and they had all the proper papers with them. They spoke little, since this was forbidden.

At the first post, the warden looked at them as though they were out of their minds, and they became confused. But the senior guard produced the order which said that the prisoner was a secret one and had no figure, after which the warden got busy and assigned to them a special cell with three cots for the night. He avoided conversing with them and was so obsequious that the guards involuntarily began to feel their own importance.

When they approached the second outpost—a much larger one—it was with confidence and an air of silent dignity. The older guard simply threw the order down on the commandant's desk, and, like the first man, he too fawned on them and bustled away to accommodate them.

Little by little they came to realize that they were escorting a most important prisoner. They became accustomed to the situation and spoke significantly to each other of their charge as "he" or "it."

They had already come deep into the heartland of the Russian Empire, along the straight, well-trodden Vladimir Road.

And the empty space which patiently marched between them changed constantly: now it was wind, now dust, now the weary, thoroughly exhausted heat of late summer.

13.

Meanwhile, an important order followed them along the same Vladimir Road, from tollgate to tollgate, from fortress to fortress.

Yury Alexandrovich Neledinsky-Meletsky had said "Wait." And he was not mistaken.

For the great fear of Paul Petrovich was slowly but surely giving way to melting sentiment and tender pity for himself.

The Emperor had turned away from the beast-like garden shrubbery, and, after wandering for a while in emptiness, he turned his face to Cameron's delicate sensibilities.

He had broken the backs of his mother's governors and generals; he had sent them off to their estates, where they were sitting it out. He had to do it. And what was the result? A huge vacuum had formed around him.

He had put up a box for letters and complaints before his palace, for it was he and no one else who was the father of his land. At first the box remained empty, and this grieved him, for the land should speak to its father. Later an unsigned letter was found in the box; it called him pug-nosed daddy and threatened him.

He looked at himself in the mirror.

"Pug-nosed, my dear sirs, pug-nosed indeed," he wheezed and ordered the box removed.

He set out on a journey across this strange land. He exiled to Siberia the governor who had dared to build new bridges in his province for the Emperor's crossings. The journey was not like his mama's journeys: everything had to be just as it always was; nothing was to be prettied up.[5] However, the land was silent. Near the Volga, some peasants gathered around him. He sent a young fellow to dip some water for him from the middle of the river, so that he would have clean water to drink.

He drank the water and said gruffly to the peasants:

"Well, here I am, drinking your water. What're you gaping at?"

And the space around him became empty.

He never undertook another journey. And, instead of a complaint box, he set up strong guard units at every outpost. But he never knew whether they were loyal, and never knew who was to be feared and suspected.

He was surrounded by treason and emptiness.

He had found the secret of eradicating them: he introduced absolute precision and subordination. His many offices went to work. For himself, he assumed only executive power. But somehow it happened that the executive power threw all the offices into confusion, and therefore there was nothing around but dubious treason, emptiness, and a sly pretense at subordination. He saw himself as a chance swimmer lifting up his bare hands among raging waves; he had seen such an engraving once.

And yet, he was, after many long years, the sole legitimate Monarch.

And he was burdened with the desire to lean on his father, even a dead father. He exhumed from the grave the German imbecile[6] who had been murdered with a fork and who was considered to have been his father, and placed his coffin next to the coffin of the usurper of the throne. But this was done mostly to avenge himself on his dead mother, during whose lifetime he had lived as a man condemned to momentary execution.

Besides, was she really his mother?

He knew something vaguely about the scandal attending his birth.

He was a homeless orphan, deprived of even a dead father, even a dead mother.

He never thought about all this and would have ordered any man who suspected him of such thoughts shot out of a cannon.

Yet at such moments he was ready to take pleasure in the slightest jest, the most foolish prank, and in the little Chinese houses of his Trianon. He became a simple friend of nature and wanted to be loved by everyone, or at least by someone.

This usually came upon him in fits, and then rudeness was regarded as frankness, stupidity as directness, cunning as goodness, and the Turkish orderly who shined his boots became a Count.

Yury Alexandrovich always felt the changes with some sixth sense.

He had waited a week, and then he sensed it.

With quiet but jaunty steps he approached the glass screen, shifted from foot to foot, and suddenly told the Emperor, under the guise of candor, all that he knew about Second Lieutenant Nants—with the exception, naturally, of the pug-nosed gesture.

The Emperor burst into a barking, dog-like, hoarse and broken laugh, as though he were trying to frighten someone.

Yury Alexandrovich became alarmed.

He had wanted to do Nelidova a favor, as her household friend, and also, in the meantime, to demonstrate his own importance—for, according to the German proverb current at the time, "*umsonst ist der Tod*"—only death is free. But such laughter could drive Yury Alexandrovich without delay into the grave. It could prove the instrument of his undoing.

Was the Emperor sarcastic?

But no, the Emperor was faint from so much laughter. He stretched his hand for the pen, and Yury Alexandrovich, raising himself on tiptoe, read as the Emperor's hand wrote:

"Second Lieutenant Nants, exiled to Siberia, is to be returned, promoted to Lieutenant, and married to the Maid-in-Waiting."

After he had written these words, the Emperor strode across the room, elated and inspired.

He clapped his hands and began his favorite song, singing and whistling:

> "O my fir trees, my green fir trees,
> my sweet shining birch grove."

And Yury Alexandrovich echoed in a thin, small voice:

> "Liushenki, lullee . . ."

14.

A bitten dog runs off into the field and cures himself there with bitter herbs.

Lieutenant Sinukhayev went on foot from St. Petersburg to Gatchina. He was going to his father—not in order to ask for help, but perhaps simply because he wanted to see for himself whether there was really a father in Gatchina. Perhaps there was no father there at all. He did not reply to his father's greeting, but looked around and prepared to leave, like a shy man, or one who liked to be asked twice.

But the surgeon, seeing his tattered clothing, made him sit down and began to question him:

"Did you lose at cards, or were you punished for something?"

"I am not alive," the Lieutenant said suddenly.

The surgeon felt his pulse, said something about leeches, and persisted with his questions.

When he learned about his son's negligence, he became agitated and spent a whole hour writing and rewriting a petition. Then he made his son sign it and took it on the following day to Baron Arakcheyev, to be submitted with his daily report. Nevertheless, he felt constrained about keeping his son at home, and placed him instead in the infirmary, where he wrote on the board above his bed:

> *Mors occasionalis*
> (Accidental death)

15.

Baron Arakcheyev was troubled by the idea of the state.

Therefore his character was difficult to define, it was elusive. The Baron was not vindictive; indeed, at times he was even gracious and condescending. When he heard a sad story, it moved him to tears, like a child. And he often gave the girl who tended his garden a kopek as he strolled along the path. Then, noticing that the paths were not well swept, he would order the girl whipped. After the punishment, he gave the child a five-kopek piece.

In the presence of the Emperor he felt a certain faintness resembling love.

He worshiped cleanliness; it was the very emblem of his temper. But he was happy only when he found faults in cleanliness and order. When there were none, he was secretly grieved. And instead of fresh roast, he always ate salt beef.

He was absent-minded like a philosopher. And, indeed, learned Germans found a certain resemblance between his eyes and the eyes of the philosopher Kant, well-known in Germany at the time: they were of a pale indefinite color, as though veiled by a transparent film. But the Baron took offense when someone spoke to him of this resemblance.

He was miserly, but he loved to make a flourish and present everything in the best light. To this end, he entered into the smallest details. He pored over plans for chapels, medals, icons, and dining tables. He was fascinated by circles, ellipses, and lines that were interlaced like strips of leather in a whip, producing patterns capable of deceiving the eye. And he was fond of hoodwinking a visitor, or even the Emperor, but pretended not to notice when anyone succeeded in fooling him as well. But then, it was not easy to put anything over on him.

He kept a detailed inventory of the belongings of each of his servants, from his chamber valet to the small boy who served as the cook's helper. He also maintained a careful check on all the infirmary inventories.

During the construction of the hospital where the father of Lieutenant Sinukhayev was employed, the Baron himself directed the placement of the beds, the benches, and the surgeon's desk; he even decided on the kind of pen to be used: it was to be bare, tuftless, like a Roman *calamus*, or reed. If the assistant surgeon failed to remove the tufts in trimming the pen, he was subject to a penalty of five strokes with a birch rod.

Baron Arakcheyev was preoccupied with the idea of the Roman state.

Therefore, he listened absently to surgeon Sinukhayev, and it was only when the latter handed him the petition that he gave it his attention and reprimanded the surgeon because the signature was illegible.

The surgeon apologized, saying that his son's hand trembled.

"Ah, my friend, you see," the Baron replied with satisfaction. "His hand trembled."

Then he glanced at the surgeon and asked:

"And when did the death occur?"

"On June 15th," the surgeon answered, somewhat taken aback.

"June 15th," the Baron drawled, thinking. "June 15th . . . And today is already the 17th," he suddenly said straight into the surgeon's face. "And where was the corpse for two days?"

He grinned at the surgeon's expression, then glanced dourly at the petition and said:

"Rank mismanagement! And now good-bye, sir, be off with you."

16.

The singer and State Secretary Meletsky took risks, and often he won, because he presented everything in the most delicate manner, matching Cameron's hues. But winnings alternated with losses, as in the game of quadrille.

Baron Arakcheyev's method was different. He took no risks and guaranteed nothing. On the contrary, in his reports to the Emperor, he pointed out abuses—there they are!—and begged for instructions on how to eliminate them. Meletsky risked disfavor. The Baron humbled himself in advance. But then, the possible winnings looming in the distance were greater, as in the game of faro.

The Baron dryly reported to the Emperor that the deceased Lieutenant Sinukhayev had arrived in Gatchina, where he was duly placed in the infirmary. He had, moreover, declared himself alive and submitted a petition for reinstatement in the rosters. Which petition was hereby transmitted, with a request for further instructions. The Baron had meant to show his subordination by submitting this paper—like a zealous steward who consulted his master in all matters.

The reply came promptly, both to the petition and to Baron Arakcheyev himself.

The petition was marked by the resolution:

"Request of the late Lieutenant Sinukhayev, separated from the rosters by reason of death, denied for the same reason."

As for Baron Arakcheyev, he received the following note:

"Sir, Baron Arakcheyev,

"I am astonished that, though holding the rank of General, you are ignorant of the regulations, bringing directly to me the petition of the deceased Lieutenant Sinukhayev, who, moreover, does not even belong to your regiment, and which should properly have been referred first to the office of the Lieutenant's regiment, instead of troubling me directly by said petition.

"Nevertheless, I remain, favorably inclined,

Paul"

The letter did not say "as ever favorably inclined." And Arakcheyev shed some tears, since he mortally disliked receiving reprimands. He went personally to the infirmary and ordered the deceased Lieutenant turned out immediately, after issuing him a set of underwear. As for his officer's uniform, listed in the inventory, it was to be detained.

17.

By the time Second Lieutenant Nants returned from Siberia, many people knew about him. He was the officer who had cried "Help!" under the Emperor's window, who had been punished and exiled to Siberia, and later pardoned and promoted to Lieutenant. Such were the entirely definite features of his life.

The Commander no longer felt any constraint with him and simply assigned him, now to guard duty, now to other tasks. When the regiment left town for maneuvers in camp, the Lieutenant went with it. He was considered a good officer, for nothing wrong had ever been noted about him.

The Maid-in-Waiting whose brief faint had saved him was at first overjoyed, thinking that she was about to be reunited with her vanished lover. She pasted a beauty spot on her cheek and tightened the laces of her gown, which would not quite come together. But later, in church, she noticed that she stood alone, while an adjutant held the marriage crown over the empty space next to her. She was just about to fall into another faint, but, as her eyes were lowered and she saw her waistline, she thought better of it. Many of the guests were quite impressed with the somewhat mysterious ceremony, from which the bridegroom was absent.

Some time later, a son was born to Lieutenant Nants—an image of his father, according to rumor.

The Emperor forgot about him. He had much to occupy him.

The lively Nelidova was retired, giving place to the plump Gagarina. Cameron, the Swiss chalets, and even all of Pavlovskoye were forgotten. The soldierly St. Petersburg lay spread out in its squat, brick regularity. Suvorov[7], whom the Emperor disliked but tolerated because he had been the enemy of the late Potemkin, was disturbed out of his rustic retirement. A military campaign was in the offing, since the Emperor had plans. These plans were numerous, and often they overleaped each other with confusing rapidity. Paul Petrovich expanded in girth and seemed to have grown shorter. His face was now altogether brick-colored. Suvorov fell into disfavor once more. The Emperor laughed more and more infrequently.

One day, scanning the regimental rosters, he came across Lieutenant Nants' name and raised him to the rank of captain. Another time he promoted him to colonel. The Lieutenant was a model officer. Then the Emperor forgot about him again.

Colonel Nants' life flowed by imperceptibly, and everyone accepted this. At home he had his own study, in the barracks, his own room, and sometimes reports and orders were brought there, without too much wonder at the Colonel's absence.

He was already in command of a regiment.

But happiest of all was the Maid-in-Waiting in her huge double bed. Her husband was advancing in the service, the bed was comfortable, her son growing. On occasion, the Colonel's conjugal place was warmed by some lieutenant, captain, or civilian. This, however, was true of many a colonel's bed in St. Petersburg, whose owner was away on campaign.

Once, when the wearied lover slept, she heard a creaking in the next room. The creaking was repeated. It must have been a floor board, drying out. But she instantly shook the sleeping man awake and flung his clothes out after him through the door. When she recovered her composure, she laughed at herself.

But this too happened in many a colonel's home.

18.

The peasants smelled of wind, the women of smoke.

Lieutenant Sinukhayev never looked anyone in the face and distinguished people by smell.

By smell he chose his resting places at night, trying to sleep under a tree, because the rain would wet him less under its shelter.

He walked on, without stopping anywhere.

He passed through Finnish villages leaving as little trace as a flat pebble sent skimming over the surface of the water by a boy. Sometimes a Finnish woman would give him some milk. He drank it, standing, and went on. Children grew quiet, the whitish drippings under their noses glistening as they watched him. The village would close up behind him.

His gait changed little. From so much walking it became still more unstrung. But still this flabby, loose-jointed, almost toylike gait remained the gait of an officer, a military man.

He took no notice of direction. And yet the direction could be traced. Veering this way and that, zigzagging like the lightning in pictures of the Flood, he circled around and around, and these circles constantly grew smaller.

A year went by, and then the circle shrank to a dot; he reached St. Petersburg and walked around it from end to end.

Then he began to circle within the city, and sometimes would go round and round in the same path for weeks.

He walked quickly, with the same military, unstrung gait which made his hands and feet seem only loosely attached.

The shopkeepers hated him.

Whenever he passed along Gostiny Ryad, they shouted after him:

"Come yesterday!"

"Play backward!"

It was said that he brought bad luck, and the women who sold bread in the streets would slip him a bun to ward off his evil eye.

Street urchins who have ever been adept at capturing a weak point, ran after him, shouting:

"Dangle-doll!"

19.

In St. Petersburg the guards around the castle of Paul Petrovich cried out:

"The Emperor is sleeping!"

The cry was taken up by the halberdiers at the crossings:

"The Emperor is sleeping!"

And like a windstorm, this cry caused shops to close one after the other, and pedestrians to hide in their homes.

It signaled the coming of night.

On St. Isaac's Square, the groups of peasants clad in homespun, who had been herded into the city from their villages for work, put out their bonfires and settled down on the ground where they stood, pulling their ragged jerkins over them.

After crying out that "The Emperor is sleeping!" the guards armed with halberds fell asleep themselves. A sentry paced back and forth like a clock atop the Fortress of Peter and Paul. In one of the taverns on the outskirts of town a fellow girdled with a strip of bast sat drinking royal wine with a coachman.

"The pug-nosed daddy hasn't got much time left," said the coachman. "I drove some important gentlemen. . . . "

The drawbridge at the castle was raised, and Paul Petrovich looked out of the window.

For the moment he was safe on his island.

But there were looks and whispers in the palace which he understood quite well, and in the streets the people dropped to their knees before his horse with a strange expression. This was a custom he had introduced, but now people dropped into the mud differently, not as before. They dropped too hastily. His horse was tall, and he swayed in the saddle. He was reigning too fast. The castle was not sufficiently protected; it was too spacious. He must select a smaller room. However, Paul Petrovich was unable to do so—it would immediately be noticed. "If I could crawl into the snuffbox," thought the Emperor, snuffing the tobacco. He did not light the candle. He must not show where he was. He stood in the dark, in his underwear. By the window, he took account of his people. He shifted them, he crossed Bennigsen out of his memory and entered Olsufiev.

The list did not tally.

"My reckoning isn't. . . . "

"Arakcheyev is a fool," he said in an undertone.

" . . . the vague incertitude with which he tries to please. . . . "

The sentry could be faintly seen by the drawbridge.

"It's necessary," Paul Petrovich said by force of habit.

He tapped his fingers on the snuffbox.

"It's necessary," he tried to remember, tapping, and suddenly stopped.

Everything that was necessary had long been done, and proved insufficient.

"Alexander Pavlovich[8] must be imprisoned," he said hurriedly, and waved his hand.

"It's necessary. . . . "

What was necessary?

He lay down and slipped under the quilt, as quickly as he did everything else.

He fell fast asleep.

At seven in the morning he awakened as though someone had jolted him, and suddenly remembered: it was necessary to elevate and bring close to himself some simple and modest man who would owe everything to him, and to dismiss all others.

And he fell asleep again.

20.

In the morning Paul Petrovich looked over the orders. Colonel Nants was promoted to general. He was a colonel who did not importune him with requests for land; he did not try to gain advancement on the strength of an uncle's high position; he was not a braggart or a blusterer. He did his duty without complaint or fuss.

Paul Petrovich demanded to see his service record. He halted over the paper that showed that in his early days, as a lieutenant, the Colonel had been exiled to Siberia for crying "Help!" under the Emperor's window. He recalled something vaguely and smiled. There had been some light amorous adventure.

How much he needed now a man who at the proper moment would cry "Help!" under his window. He granted General Nants an estate with a thousand serfs.

In the evening of that day General Nants' name came to the fore. It was on everybody's lips.

Someone had heard the Emperor say to Count Pahlen with a smile that had not been seen for quite some time:

"Wait to burden him with a division. I need him for more important things."

No one but Bennigsen was willing to admit that he knew nothing about the General. Pahlen squinted and kept his silence.

The First Gentleman of the Chamber Alexander Lvovich Naryshkin recalled the General:

"Oh, yes, Colonel Nants . . . I remember. He ran after Sandunova. . . . "

"At the maneuvers near Krasnoye. . . . "

"I remember, a kinsman of Olsufiev, Fyodor Yakovlevich. . . . "

"He is no kinsman of Olsufiev, Count. Colonel Nants is from France. His father was beheaded by the mob in Toulon."

21.

Events moved quickly. General Nants was summoned to the Emperor. On the same day it was reported to the Emperor that the General had fallen dangerously ill.

He grunted with chagrin and twisted a button off the coat of Count Pahlen who had brought the news.

He muttered hoarsely:

"Take him to the hospital and have him cured. And if they do not cure him, sir. . . . "

The Emperor's *Valet de Chambre* visited the hospital twice daily to inquire about General Nants' health.

In the large ward, behind tightly shut doors, the surgeons bustled about, shivering as though they were patients themselves.

By the evening of the third day General Nants was dead.

Paul Petrovich was no longer angry. He looked at everybody with a foggy eye and withdrew to his chamber.

22.

General Nants' funeral was long remembered by St. Petersburg, and certain memoirs preserved its details.

The regiment marched with furled flags. Thirty court carriages, empty and filled, swayed behind.

Such was the will of the Emperor. Medals and decorations were carried after the coffin on cushions.

Behind the heavy black coffin walked the General's widow, leading her child by the hand.

She was crying.

As the procession filed past the castle, Paul Petrovich slowly rode out by himself upon the bridge to watch it and raised his unsheathed sword.

"My best men are dying."

Then, after the court carriages had rolled by, he said in Latin, following them with his eyes:

"*Sic transit gloria mundi.*"

23.

And so General Nants was buried, having fulfilled all that can be fulfilled in life, having experienced youth and amorous adventure, punishment and exile, years of service, family life, the sudden favor of the Emperor, and the envy of the courtiers.

His name was duly entered in the "St. Petersburg Necropolis" and later mentioned in passing by several historians.

The "St. Petersburg Necropolis" contains no mention of the dead Lieutenant Sinukhayev.

He vanished without a trace, scattered to dust, to chaff, as though he had never existed.

And Paul Petrovich died in March of the same year as General Nants, of apoplexy—according to the official record.

Young Vitushishnikov

Cast of Characters

Historical:

Emperor Nicholas I. Born in 1796, third son of the Emperor Paul, succeeded to the Russian throne upon the sudden death of his elder brother, Alexander I. Reigned 1825-1855. With little education except in military matters, lacking in intelligence and initiative, incompetent, and given to meddling in details. Pompous, vain, cold, full of self-adulation and self-pity.

His accession was greeted by the Decembrist Uprising, organized by a group of aristocratic Guards officers influenced by Western ideas, who led out their regiments on December 14th to protest against the reactionary autocracy and demand a constitution. The uprising was quelled. Five of the leaders were hanged, although Alexander had abolished the death penalty. Others were exiled to hard labor in Siberia, sentenced to prison terms, or demoted to service in the ranks.

Nelidova, Varvara (Varenka) Arkadievna (? - 1897). Maid-in-Waiting at the court, the Emperor's favorite.

Count Orlov, Alexey Fyodorovich (1786 - 1861). Enjoyed the Emperor's favor for his role in suppressing the Decembrist Uprising. From 1844 to 1856, head of the notorious Third Section of His Imperial Majesty's Own Chancery, established by Nicholas in 1826 as the highest office of the political police, and Chief of the Gendarmerie, the security police attached to the Third Section.

Kleinmichel, Pyotr Andreyevich (1793 - 1869). Adjutant-General, Chief Superintendent of Engineering, Transportation, and Public Buildings. Won the Emperor's fullest trust by slavishly obeying every order. Given a number of decorations and awards, including the title of Count. Appointed Director of Railway Construction, to link Petersburg and Moscow, although he had never seen either a railway car or a locomotive.

Dame Kleinmichel, his wife.

Vronchenko, Fyodor Pavlovich (1780 - 1852). Privy Councillor. Appointed Minister of Finance in 1844. Followed in the footsteps of his reactionary predecessor, Kankrin.

Levashov, Vasily Vasilievich (1783 - 1848). Adjutant-General, Chairman of the State Council and the Committee of Ministers.

Panin, Victor Nikitich (1801 - 1874). Minister of Justice, 1841 - 1862.

Bulgarin, Faddey Venediktovich (1789 - 1859). Writer, journalist, publisher of the reactionary newspaper *The Northern Bee* and the journal *Son of* *the Fatherland* (with N.I. Grech). From 1826 an active agent of the secret political police, who kept the authorities informed about his fellow writers. Enemy of Pushkin and butt of the poet's crushing epigrams.

Fictional:

Old gendarmes.

Two soldiers of the Carbine Company of the Chasseurs Life Guards Regiment.

Customs officials.

Yakov, the Emperor's coachman.

Lieutenant Koshkul 2nd.

Young Vitushishnikov.

Collegial Registrar Vitushishnikov, father of young Vitushishnikov.

Mistress of the tavern.

Konaki, wine-merchant, vintner, and concessionaire.

Konaki sons.

Rodokanaki, Commercial Councillor, concessionaire and great merchant.

Director of the Department of Public Buildings.

Young Maid-in-Waiting.

Three Court Chamberlains.

Kleinmichel's sister.

Kammer-Frau Baranova.

Maids-in-Waiting, her charges.

N. Shubinsky, a historian.

Veteran guard.

Courtiers, people in the street, gentry and simple folk, driving, walking, running, gaping.

Scene:

St. Petersburg, in the late 1840s.

The Imperial Court and Palace in St. Petersburg.

Barracks of the Chasseurs Life Guards Regiment in an unprepossessing district of the city.

Drinking Establishment in the same district.

Nevsky Prospect.

Customs House.

Mansion of Rodokanaki, concessionaire and great merchant.

Quarters of the Maids-in-Waiting in the Palace.

Home for Indigent Children.

Young Vitushishnikov's new house.

The Emperor's "campaign" office, where the reconciliation takes place.

1.

The night was restless. Twice he arose and cast a stern glance around the room. Then he said:

"So!"

And, wrapping himself in a field coat, he instantly fell asleep.

He lay on a narrow campaign bed. There was no campaign, but some evenings he withdrew to the solitude of a special "campaign" chamber, his "field office," and there he went to sleep, wrapped in a coarse gray soldier's coat.

It was noted that such withdrawals usually took place after days when he had been burdened by family or state affairs.

And yesterday had been just such a day: Varvara Arkadievna Nelidova had banished the Emperor from her affections.

After a night on the campaign bed, he usually arose filled with resolution. He washed himself with cold water, like a common soldier, rubbed his muscles, and spent several seconds stroking the area where the barrier between the chest and abdomen was supposed to be. The suggestion of the court physician Mandt, to remove excess. Then he dressed rapidly, and made a sudden appearance.

And so it was this day. Breakfast passed splendidly. He patted the Heir with gracious words. Then he proceeded to the telegraph room. A year ago the first electro-magnetic telegraph had been installed, connecting his Winter Palace with three necessary persons: the Chief of the Gendarmerie Orlov, the Chief Superintendent of Engineering, Kleinmichel, and the Maid-in-Waiting Nelidova who resided on the Fontanka. The telegraph was the invention of the learned official on the staff of the Third Section, Baron Schilling von Kapstadt. Eschewing the ordinary alphabet, the Emperor preferred his own code system—*le système Nicolas.* Sending the telegraph officer out of the room, he dispatched his own special word to the Maid-in-Waiting Nelidova, which signified *"Barbe."*

Although the message had most probably reached its destination, there was no reply.

He repeated:

"Barbe."

Then, hastily and aggrieved, he sent at once:

"Are you still offended?"

Soon the electro-magnetic apparatus received the reply:

"Your Majesty . . . "

The usual form, for the sake of brevity, was "Sire."

" . . . grant me leave . . . "

The Emperor, armed with a long pencil, decoded the meaning.

" . . . to retire. . . . "

He put down his pencil.

With a light sigh, he frowned, and the telegrams were done with for the day.

After that, the audience, and hearing of various affairs of state.

2.

The quarrel had occurred for the following reason.

Being a paragon, being exemplary by very virtue of his position, the Emperor desired one thing: to be surrounded by models of perfection. Varenka Nelidova not only had a stately figure and regular features, but she also, as it were, provided the Emperor with assurance that everything around was developing and moving forward with giant strides. She was the niece of his father's favorite, another Maid-in-Waiting Nelidova, which both justified him as a man, and offered a comparison unfavorable to the past epoch. The earlier Nelidova was small, swarthy, homely, and given to contradictions. The present one was of serene, splendid stature, with limbs of marble pallor, and with that smallness of head in relation to the body which the Emperor regarded as the effect and the token of breeding.

Several days ago, during her usual presentation to the Emperor, she suddenly buried her face in his chest and declared that she was with child. This was as much a family matter as a matter of state.

As a man, the Emperor was pleasantly surprised. On that day he jested benevolently, lightly signed the state balance, suddenly conferred the Order of St. Catherine upon Dame Kleinmichel (a relation), and succeeded in every endeavor. Then his thoughts turned to the future coat of arms and certain steps to be undertaken. For the coat of arms he envisioned an oval pale blue field and three golden fish. The title—Duke, or better, Count. The surname was still to be chosen. Of those that suggested themselves, three appeared suitable: Nikolayev, Romanovsky, Nelidovsky. That the child might be a daughter, of female gender, never occurred to him. Then he considered the mother's regimen. She must take a daily stroll in the Apollo Hall or the Hermitage for not less than an hour. Surrounded on all sides by statues, seeing around her the marble torsos and columns, being thus herself the center of elegance, the young mother must necessarily produce only the elegant.

But soon the Emperor was somewhat carried away in his cogitations. His mind that evening dwelling solely on matters relating to woman and her mission, he vividly imagined the events to come and pictured his first welcome to the infant.

He saw the rosy infant presented to him by the wet-nurse, and himself, true to the custom of the simple Russian folk, placing his gifts to the newborn on the cushion—a little scroll, with the coat of arms and all the rest of it.

Presented by the festively attired nurse. . . . And imperceptibly, in passing, as it were, he recalled the affair of the uniform costumes of the Maids-in-Waiting, and he frowned. The matter of the women's formal costumes was never successfully resolved and caused much talk. At this point, his thought returned to the nurses. And he realized with astonishment that, even at the very highest levels, they had no uniforms at all. Total disarray, including impossible loose floppy blouses and kerchiefs. The next day he ordered Kleinmichel to call in artists to sketch the designs. Kleinmichel acted promptly. Two days later the artists submitted their ideas.

For the head, the traditional *kokoshnik*, framing the smoothly combed hair and tied in the back with the large bow of a wide ribbon, its two ends hanging down as low as desired. A *sarafan* with gold lacework. Embroidered sleeves.

The artists vowed that a buxom nurse in this uniform, with her massive yet harmonious proportions, would put anyone else in the shade.

The uniform met with the Emperor's approval. He merely instructed that care be taken to introduce a sharper distinction between it and the formal costume of the Maids-in-Waiting, which was also in peasant style. And it was this very uniform that had caused the rift.

Varenka Nelidova was suddenly besieged with congratulations, and the affair received the widest publicity.

The question of the nurses' uniform was temporarily set aside, but the chill was still in force, for the third day now.

3.

Crossing the Apollo Hall, he caught sight of himself for a moment in a mirror, with a copy of Phoebus behind him. And involuntarily he halted, overcome with a strong sense of his melancholy greatness: the Emperor, his feelings bitterly rebuffed, on his way to the St. George Hall to receive his soldiers. And, reaching the St. George Hall, he instantly assumed the appropriate pose: older than usual, a man who had suffered much, the Emperor receives the parade of his aged soldiers.[1]

Presenting themselves were veteran officers of the gendarmerie. The Emperor's glance halted on the eldest. He recalled seeing him somewhere.

"Have we met somewhere before?" he asked mournfully.

"Yes, Sir, Your Majesty. I had the good fortune. Permit me to be pensioned off," said the old man, his eyes tearing.

"Wait, my old . . . drabant," said the Emperor. "We shall be pensioned off together."

Everyone started.

The Emperor wanted to say "my old comrade-in-arms," but he had no recollection whatever of where he had seen the gendarme, and so he said "old drabant," which was the designation of his palace guard. And added the words about being pensioned off.

Seeing a tear in every eye, he was pleased.

"Develop a taste for good deeds," he said.

The audience was over.

4.

Two soldiers of the Carbine Company of the Chasseurs Regiment felt the need for a drink. After ten years of soldiering, these two men, who occupied neighboring cots, each with a single penalty on his record, but neither under surveillance, developed a simultaneous thirst for some vodka. At night, turning from side to side, they confided this to each other. The undertaking was hazardous.

"Ry-ysky," said the older one, and shifted on his back.

The barracks were situated in one of the unprepossessing spots, which abounded in Petersburg. Ten minutes' walk away were government buildings, then the Neva River and the bridge connecting the Petersburg District with Vasilievsky Island— large and important installations. But all around were wooded areas, barren and dark, a tobacco shop, an almshouse, where lively veterans could be seen, and beyond that—an altogether transparent, whitish wilderness. The tavern was in the direction of the government buildings.

The older soldier worked in the regimental tailoring shop, and it was possible for him to slip out by volunteering for a delivery or some errand. The problem was with the second man. But even the second one might have a chance. The company commander used his skills as a cobbler, and he might possibly be summoned to the commander's residence to take a measure of his wife's feet.

"Ry-ysk," said the cobbler. "Can't get away from ry-ysk."

The other was troubled. Doubtful.

The men of the regiment had no spare time, with nothing to do. The time left over after drill, after tailoring and mending, cleaning of uniforms and equipment, and so on, was filled up with childish games. However, if a soldier committed a breach of regulations, the commander treated him as someone of an entirely different age. Then he was treated as a grown man. On holidays there was also an exception: the men received a glass of vodka, which was known as a "foamer" or a "good foamer," and the glass, as a "noggin." On holidays, too, the men were admitted to "the privilege of women," which was also known in the regiment as being "let out to pasture," or "to grass." Sick soldiers and those under punishment enjoyed the privilege in the infirmary.

On this particular day both soldiers were in luck.

Leaving the gates of the barracks, each on an official errand, they separated and went off in different directions. Then one waited for the other, who joined him presently. The two drew up to attention, fell into step, and proceeded, in marching tempo, to the tavern.

The hour was one in the afternoon.

5.

After a brief rest, the Emperor, obliged to attend to all aspects of subordinate life, received the Superintendent of Transportation and Public Buildings, Adjutant-General Kleinmichel.

Of medium height and very solid build, with a red moustache, just a bit thicker than the Emperor's, Count Pyotr Andreyevich Kleinmichel was a complex nature. In managing the affairs entrusted to him, he disliked signing documents, and performed all business by personal agreement and oral orders. For the sake of speed, all sums were calculated immediately, on the spot, in the presence of the person concerned. Transferred from one high post to another, he had acquired a motley education. His slogan was "diligence overcomes all obstacles." Stout, red-haired, and moustached, he had the delicate skin of a young girl. As he passed the ranks of his subordinates, he addressed them in a brisk, ringing voice and moved rapidly. In cases of a slip or a transgression, he permitted himself familiarities: he rapped the offender on the nose with his pencil. But he was also blunt in speech. In hearing reports, he openly called, say, the Finance Minister Vronchenko, a swine. Whenever that name was mentioned, he instantly commented "Swine!" and no longer listened to the report.

Yet he trembled like a boarding school girl at the very breath of the Emperor. Entering his study, he shrank in size, turned pale, his moustache drooped, and he melted visibly. He spoke in a hoarse, fervent whisper, and when he finally regained his voice, it was a thin, childish treble. The Emperor's proximity produced a purely physiological effect on Kleinmichel. When the Emperor was angry, the General was attacked by nausea. Retiring to a corner, he took some time in fighting off the spasms. The Emperor was aware of this weakness and respected him for it.

"Your own fault," he would say to the General when the latter became flustered.

This weakness was, at the same time, the strength of Adjutant-General Kleinmichel. It moved him inwardly to promptness in fulfilling the Emperor's commands pertaining to construction projects, and, on the other hand, it demonstrated his total subservience to his Sovereign's will.

He gradually learned to avoid the Emperor's displeasure. Being the general on duty, he had to present himself at the palace every morning with the latest report. His horses were faster than anyone's, which he felt to be especially important for a chief of transportation facilities. "Hell and brimstone!" was his usual order to the coachman.

Exactly at noon he arrived at the palace in his sleigh with his black briefcase, solid as a coffin.

With little steps, breathless, a carefree expression on his pink face, he made his way to the Emperor's chamber. At the threshold he turned pale.

As he clicked his heels, his spurs rang delicately. After the salutation, he immediately drew from his briefcase a variety of objects, which he laid out before the Emperor: a yellow cord, for braid, five cuts of dark green fabric for uniforms, of different shades, a little cap, especially made as a sample for the transportation department, and a tightly covered tin can, with black paint.

All these were samples.

The Emperor looked at them with an unprejudiced eye. He picked up the cord from the table and, glancing at the Count, wrapped it around his index finger. The General held up under his glance. The Emperor pulled sharply at the cord. The cord held up under the test. Slightly raising the lid of the can, the Emperor sniffed it and asked squeamishly:

"What is this?"

"Paint for the sentry boxes, Sire."

The Emperor sniffed at it again, and put it down.

"Have you readied the new estimate?"

"I have, Sire."

"How much?"

"Fifty-seven million, Your Majesty."

"Fifty-five—and not another word. My money doesn't drop from the sky."

The estimate in question had to do with the new Nikolayev railway line. The initial figure had been rejected. The work was generally conducted on the basis of market rates.

The Emperor gave Kleinmichel a stern look.

"I will command the engineers to be honest," he said. "Did you set out the curb posts?"[2]

From the building of the Customs Administration the street along the Neva River was lined with posts on one side only. On the other side, it bordered directly on the cold granite of the embankment. Striving for symmetry not only in the internal questions of state, but also in the external appearance of the capital, the Sovereign had drawn the General's attention to it as they drove past.

"They are in place, Your Majesty," the General replied in melancholy tones.

The Sovereign pointed at the cord, the tiny cap, and the can:

"Take it."

The audience was over.

6.

Leaving the palace, Count Kleinmichel got into the sleigh and shouted in a desperate voice to his well-trained coachman:

"Rush it, swine! To the office! Hell and brimstone!"

Three officers passing by on Nevsky Prospect sprang to attention. Officials of other departments removed their caps. The speed of the ride told everyone that it was Count Kleinmichel tearing along on urgent business.

He hurried to his office, looking at no one.

"Call that swine, Ignatov," he ordered.

The swine Ignatov, State Councillor,[3] appeared.

"The curb posts! Where's Yeremeyev? Fire-chief! Fire-chief!"

"Fire-chief" was the nickname of State Councillor Yeremeyev, Municipal Supervisor, whose task it was to see that the streets were properly maintained. No one knew how the nickname originated.

The point of the matter was simple; Adjutant-General Kleinmichel had forgotten to issue orders to set up the curb posts.

With a sweetish taste in his mouth—presage of the onset of nausea—General Kleinmichel was giving orders. The posts turned out to be ready, but not yet set up. In five minutes, a company of army engineers was dispatched to the work site. Every five minutes men of the exterior police arrived with reports. Everything, they said, was in order; nothing extraordinary had taken place at the site of the works in progress. Growing weaker and weaker, the General paced his office, shouting hoarsely at increasing intervals:

"I will command them to be honest!"

Within fifteen minutes the posts were erected in the requisite order, and all traces of their recent installation concealed as far as possible with crushed stone. The Emperor had not been seen at the site.

General Kleinmichel sank into his chair. "Hell and brimstone," he said.

7.

On that morning, more than ever, the Emperor felt the need for state activity. The samples, and particularly the little cap, did not please him. Not a moment was to be wasted. Should he visit the widow of the Commander of the Izmailovsky Regiment and tell the shaken maidservant:

"Announce that General Romanov is here . . . ?"

Not new. And must not be repeated more than once. He might arrange a special review of the Preobrazhensky Regiment. Or carry out a surprise inspection of the Stables Administration. Or demand to see the plans for the new Kronstadt fortress, prepared by D'Estrem. Or look into the affair of Lieutenant Matvey Glinka's abduction of a bride.

He gave orders to harness his horses and drove off to make a surprise inspection of the St. Petersburg Customs Office.

He had a thorough knowledge of the city as a strategic point. Since the unpleasant disorders that occurred on his accession, he had become accustomed to regard the various parts of the city differently. Thus, he disliked Gorokhovaya Street, he never drove along the Ekaterinhof Prospect,[4] and always held the Petersburg District in suspicion. Despite an excellent knowledge of the plan of his capital, he was nonetheless often astonished at how little the streets, in their rough natural aspect, filled with idlers and extraneous crowds, resembled the plan. He therefore preferred familiar spots—the Millionnaya, the straight, regular Nevsky Prospect, the military, orderly Field of Mars.

Vasilievsky Island he accepted for its amusing, German look. It was inhabited chiefly by bakers and apothecaries. He remembered the vaudeville in the Alexandrina Theatre, with that, what's his name . . . Karatygin, where a German was shown in a very funny light, singing in broken Russian about a police officer—

"And on the shoulder *parted* him."

He had said to Karatygin at the time—not bad, not bad at all.

"They're doing pretty good vaudevilles in the theatre today. True to life."

On the way to the Customs House, he took a drive along Nevsky.

Two officers, timid, not too smart.

Salutes, bows. At ease, at ease, gentlemen.

Ah, what a charmer! Like an hourglass, and must be pink . . . O-oh!

An excellent frost. My climate is good. The movement on Nevsky has progressed greatly. The Linden in Berlin—is it wider? No, not wider. Friedrich is an absolute fool, a pity.[5]

Bows. Whose horse is that? Zhadimirovsky's?

They're getting too free with their signs. What does it mean, "*Le dernier cri de Paris. Modes?*" Stupid. Must talk about it!

And this one? A writer? Sollogub. . . . At Elena Pavlovna's masked ball? What to do with him? Get to work, get to work, gentlemen!

An unbecoming commotion at Gostiny Dvor. Forgetting themselves. At last, recalled themselves. But that one doesn't even bow. A civilian too, the scoundrel. Who? Bows, bows. At ease, gentlemen.

Indecent, these . . . plops, *cette petarade* of horses—and . . . manure!

"Yakov! I told you—feed them refined oats!"

How stupid, those servants. God! The devil take it! Disgraceful!

Must be stricter with those . . . those boys. What are all those boys? Those messengers from the shops. They should be walking, not running.

Bows. Salutes.

And that one . . . over there. . . . What forms! At ease, at ease, child!

Coming to the bridge, he made sure the railing was properly shiny. Both cheap and handsome. He had told Kleinmichel. Reins. Air. A picture! How very pleasant this whistling sound of the sleigh in motion. Really, Kankrin is stupid. Finances cannot possibly be in bad shape. And here are the curb posts. . . . Standing. Gave orders, and here they are. Much better with them. All those people, must take them in hand. You'll answer to me, gentlemen! No one, no one can be trusted. Like that fool Friedrich —trusted, and *aufwiedersehen.* Halt!

The Customs House.

8.

He noted how the fat doorman swayed, and how his eyes blanched and faded in the instant before the man's body dropped forward in a bow. And he entered the building.

He loved the sudden fall of noise, someone's frantic whisper, and then, instant silence. And he—appears.

His eyes caught everything: the clerk behind the desk quickly crossed himself, as if searching for something by his buttons.

He ordered loudly:

"Go on with the work!"

There was the usual inspection of things, and the more ordinary the things, the clearer the sense of significance of the entire procedure. His presence lent meaning to all the objects under examination, even the most negligible. Each item was named. He took his place by the scales.

" . . . gold, women's, with a horizontal movement, made in Geneva. . . .

"Vaudeville-Cañones cigars—two cases; Dos-Amigos-Trabucco—one case. Vaudeville-Royale. . . .

"Spoons, Rococo—twelve; Renaissance handles—twelve. . . .

"Books, German, for the bookshop of Andrey Ivanov."

"Open!"

The books, he thought, were of dubious tone. He extracted two improper ones: *Katzenjammer,* a collection of dirty anecdotes, with pictures of women whose stockings could be seen beneath their skirts, and *Kartenspiel,* a manual on winning. Card games were becoming too widespread lately, which seriously troubled him. A translation of a book by Alexandre Dumas, *Countess Berthe,* was put aside as unnecessary.

Imperceptibly, he became absorbed in the examination of things. It was clear in advance that every arriving party of goods contained objects of nefarious intent. And he awaited them. At the same time there was complete uncertainty: what if nothing would be found at all?

"Candlesticks, small, for traveling—two.

"Candelabras . . .

"Cigar cases, razor cases of various sizes—ten . . .

"Wick trimmers . . . "

He stood there.

The inspection went on. Crates were opened, things extracted.

Only two cases remained, large, of solid construction.

"*Expédition officielle,*" the customs man said in an undertone.

Cases with such a designation were sent on to ministries and legations, and were not subject to examination.

He looked at the customs officials impassively.

" '*Expédition*' means you," he said. " '*Officielle*' means me. Open."

A light gasp swept the room.

They began to open cases that had for years been passed in silence by the customs men who had no right to take an interest in their contents.

"Inspect and itemize."

And now a thing occurred that had not been foreseen even by the Emperor.

"Nightgowns, ladies', silk—twenty," said the customs man.

"Quilts, silk, with tassels—five . . .

"Batiste, Girard manufacture—ten cuts . . .

"Mirrors, plate glass. . . . "

They turned frantically to the case, to verify the address. Everything was right. The load was official—*expédition officielle.* And, what in their haste they had failed to read before, it was destined for the private quarters of the Chief of Gendarmerie, Count Orlov.

"Stockings, ladies', silk—twenty pairs. . . . "

The Emperor, somewhat dazed, stood there.

Suddenly, by a wave of the hand, he halted the inspection.

"Deliver to his residence," he said.

The official nearest to him thought he had also caught the word "Vermin!" But he did not dare to hear that, and to his dying day his recollection was that the Emperor had said not "Vermin" but "Women," intended to explain the contents of the official package by the family circumstances of the Chief of Gendarmerie Count Orlov.

And the Emperor, casting a glance at everyone present, drew himself up to still greater height, and strode out in indignation with wide steps that set his large spurs ringing.

9.

The Emperor suffered from an excess of imagination.

Usually, he was not only angry, but also imagined himself being angry. He even clearly visualized, as if from outside, the entire picture and the entire significance of his anger. At the same time, his irascibility was not a simple emotion. Having formed his idea of the surrounding world in accord with the dictates of set norms, he was indignant at finding it different. But, as he understood to what extent all those around were inferior to him, he had, in essence, nothing against their having weaknesses.

Nevertheless, the incident concerning Count Orlov perplexed him.

Proceeding to the Customs House, he thought he would discover some malfeasance, without clearly imagining what it might be. He knew that the Chief of Gendarmerie took large bribes and had even appropriated someone's gold mines. But he tolerated this in view of the enormous, purely political dimensions of the sums involved. But here those quilts and the twenty duty-free nightgowns astonished him, so to speak, by the domestic concreteness of the objects. What did he need twenty nightgowns for? A thousand pigs!

He disliked being puzzled. His nostrils were distended. Emerging into the now completely deserted street, he walked to the corner. The coachman, Yakov, drove slowly after him, keeping his distance. Before stepping off the sidewalk toward the sleigh, the Emperor, giving vent to his irritation, kicked the nearest curb post.

Many historians have remarked on the fact that there are days when everything seems extraordinarily firm, with each part wonderfully fitted to the rest, and the entire course of world history rock-solid. And, on the contrary, there are days when everything is simply falling apart. The post, which the Emperor kicked in his troubled mood, suddenly keeled over on its side. The coachman on his seat grunted with surprise. The street was empty.

"Where's that scoundrel Kleinmichel?" the Emperor asked himself, staring straight at the coachman.

But Yakov was well-trained and never answered questions concerning state matters.

He quietly uttered, as always in such cases, "Um-ph" (or even "Uph"), and slightly tightened the reins, so that the word, if it was a word, could be thought to be addressed to the horses.

Yet the question was of profound importance, which became manifest in time.

If Kleinmichel had been on hand at the moment, everything would have simmered down, at least in part, as it always did in such cases. The General could have blamed the ground, or placed the company of engineers on trial. But now, facing the Neva, the nearby bridge built by D'Estrem, the Petersburg District beyond it, and the curb post at his feet, the Emperor fumed with rage, which had no outlet.

In purely pictorial terms, his face, with its rapid play of emotions, was reminiscent at such moments of the lightning in "The Death of Pompeii," painted by Brullov and "The Brass Dragon" by Bruni.

He felt as he had once on the battlefield—at Eni-bazaar[6] —when the War Council had requested his withdrawal from the field of action due to the danger of being encircled, as Peter the Great had been on the banks of the Prut. Full of bitterness over the waste of his rage, he stepped into the sleigh and commanded:

"Across the bridge, to the Petersburg District. The rounds!"

The sleigh sped forward.

"We shall see, we shall see, gentlemen scoundrels!"

The time was one in the afternoon.

10.

At this moment, having received inaccurate reports on the Emperor's movements toward Vasilievsky Island, the Chief of St. Petersburg Police, General Kokoshkin, drove out to cut across his route, attended by the chief and three officers of the Exterior Police Department. Fifteen minutes later, although he saw nothing suspicious on the way, General Kokoshkin had nevertheless detailed one of the officers, Lieutenant Koshkul 2nd, to make the rounds of the Petersburg District as well, in the direction of the barracks of the Chasseurs Regiment.

11.

Events moved quickly.

The Petersburg District, with its unpaved streets and multitude of vacant lots impassable to traffic, had its advantages: sparse population, small houses which opened to the eye a wide perspective, and absence of crowds in the streets. The sleigh, commanded by the expert coachman, flew along.

They frightened a water-carrier's nag, which nearly broke into a gallop, splashing water from the barrel. Two beggar women dived out of sight, street scenes of common people's lives flashed by, then barren tracts, and the sentry box of the city guard, soon left behind.

At this moment the Emperor caught sight, at a turn, not far from the Neva, of two soldiers in uniforms, he thought, of the Chasseurs Regiment. The soldiers, walking briskly in the clear winter air, did not hear the sound of the sleigh, and both at once stepped through a low door into a house that did not look like any of the military buildings. As he drove past the door, the Emperor read the sign, "Drinking Establishment," and, written in chalk on the fence next to it, "Tavern."

There was no doubt of it. Two men of the Chasseurs Life Guards Regiment or, in any case, of some Guards Regiment, having absented themselves heaven knows how, had entered a tavern.

This was an infraction that demanded personal intervention.

Whenever an infraction had been initiated, but not yet enacted, or, at least, not yet brought to its culmination, the duty of the command was to check or cut it short.

But if it had already begun, it was essential to halt it at the stage at which it was discovered, to prevent it from progressing further.

In this case, however, although it involved a visit to a tavern which had just been initiated and had, at any rate, not yet attained its completion, such measures were not sufficient. It was necessary to restore order, expose the culprits, and return the situation to what it had been prior to the infraction.

The disposition of the points at this time was as follows: V — vacant lot; B — sentry box of the city guards; T — tavern; and S — the Emperor's sleigh, with the coachman and the Emperor himself, who had stopped the sleigh but had not yet emerged from it.

The Emperor called out in a loud voice in the direction of B — the sentry box.

"Gua-ard!"

During duty hours each sentry box had to be manned by three guards. One, by turns, stood by the box, in uniform and armed with a halberd. A second one was considered the relief man, and the third rested.

As luck would have it, that morning the armed guard had turned his post over to one of the others who was now resting. And the relief man had stepped out on some private errand.

The situation was further complicated by the fact that the Emperor noticed some idlers on the formerly deserted street, although at a considerable distance.

One was an impassive Finn with an empty milk jug. Also, two gaping peasant women, and a very young, rosy-faced adolescent boy.

"Guard!" the Emperor called in a metallic voice.

At this moment the youth suddenly broke away from the cluster of simple folk and ran with quick steps to the sleigh.

"Allow me the happiness to call the guards, Your Majesty," he said brightly.

The Emperor gestured his assent, but also started from the sleigh, so abruptly that the coachman had not managed to unfasten the lap rug in time, and it was raised at the last moment by the youth, who happened to be there.

12.

Having entered the drinking establishment, the soldiers of the Carbine Company behaved like men settling down to relax and have a drink, or, as the lower ranks put it, a pick-me-up.

They politely asked the mistress of the tavern for two glasses of vodka, a slice of bread for each man, salt, and smoked fish.

The mistress, a plump, lively woman, proceeded expertly to slice the bread, while the soldiers sat down by the window and readied themselves for a talk. One of them, as is customary in such cases, looked out through the steamy glass, without any further thought, but nevertheless observing the street, just in case.

Suddenly there flashed in the window, on the right, a horse's head, a shiny bit, a coachman's hat, and the point of a helmet.

"Police inspector!" the soldier just managed to cry out.

13.

Flinging the door wide open, the Emperor strode over to the counter and glanced silently, as though equating them with his eye, at the tavern-keeper, the keg with its copper faucet, and the edibles on the counter, the names of which he did not know. That was enough.

As if struck by a bullet, the woman dropped at the Emperor's feet, her body doubled over, sobbing and trying to kiss the shiny boots on his small feet.

"Scum," said the Emperor.

"Don't destroy me, little father," she begged.

"Scum," the Emperor repeated. " Don't you know you're not permitted to have men in the service here?

"What can I do with them, the devils," the woman sobbed. "Don't ruin me. I have nobody here, and never had."

With the tip of his toe the Emperor flung her away. Then, somewhat recovering himself, he looked around him. The wallpaper was either marbled in design or covered with natural mold. There were three tables in the room, with stained tablecloths. A bad picture on the wall, depicting an abduction from a harem. On the counter, an array of glasses, a keg with a copper faucet, sliced bread, and some edibles, the names of which he did not know.

There were no soldiers.

14.

At a brisk pace, smartly drawn up, the youth returned to the sleigh, but did not find the Emperor.

He turned to the coachman, Yakov, and, pointing respectfully at the open tavern door, he asked:

"Are they there?"

The cautious Yakov first uttered, tightening the reins, "Umph" or "Uph," but seeing, on the one hand, that the circumstances were indeed extraordinary, and, on the other, that the youth was still under age, he answered:

"There."

"May I ask you, Sir," the youth inquired, "shall I wait for His Majesty here, or go in to report to him?"

"Wait," replied the coachman.

Then, partly out of his own curiosity, he asked without turning his head:

"And what about the guard, eh?"

"The guard is laid up with a fever. They sent for the medic," the boy answered.

"Uph," said Yakov.

Then, half-turning his head toward the youth, he examined him carefully and nodded.

"Sensible. . . . Good blood."

15.

Glancing around the drinking establishment once more, and not finding the soldiers, the Emperor stepped aside and, never bending down, looked under the tables.

No one there.

Then, totally nonplussed but refraining from further questions, he turned abruptly and walked out of the establishment.

Lieutenant Koshkul 2nd, who had just at that moment arrived on the scene, found a small crowd of people at a distance from the Emperor's sleigh, the Emperor standing near the sleigh, and a youth of medium height, bare-headed, reporting something to the Emperor.

Catching sight of Lieutenant Koshkul 2nd, the Sovereign asked with noticeable ire and animation:

"Who?"

After Lieutenant Koshkul 2nd identified himself, the Sovereign wagged a threatening finger at him and commanded:

"Surround the place."

As regards the nearby, still sparse, gathering of observers, the Emperor issued an order:

"Push back and disperse."

Then, pointing at the youth, he said:

"Reward."

At this, young Vitushishnikov, who happened to be nearby, helped His Majesty into the sleigh.

16.

Within ten minutes, Lieutenant Koshkul 2nd succeeded in bringing to the site of the incident a strong detachment of exterior police, which surrounded the area. The gathering of curious people was dispersed. All through these operations the Lieutenant kept young Vitushishnikov at his side. A careful search of the area revealed nothing suspicious, with the exception of a single drunk who had never been in military service and was identified as a St. Petersburg hurdy-gurdy player.

The tavern-keeper was interrogated on the spot, and immediately after that arrested, and the drinking establishment with all its contents was put under lock and key and sealed off. The questioning of the tavern-keeper produced little information in view of her extremely disturbed condition and the dimming of memory she complained of. Only one curious detail came to light, but Lieutenant Koshkul 2nd found it inconvenient to include it in the record.

Crying over and over that her memory was "knocked out," she kept referring to some "new one."

"When the new one came in, everything turned black."

And again:

"Even before the new one, I told them (that is, the soldiers)—it's forbidden. . . . "

Lieutenant Koshkul 2nd was finally compelled to ask the woman what *new one* she was talking about, and it turned out that she was referring to a new district police inspector who had only yesterday entered upon his duties in the Petersburg District.

Curious about this circumstance and knowing nothing about a new district police officer's visit to the tavern, Lieutenant Koshkul 2nd soon discovered that the addled tavern-keeper mistook the Emperor for a new police inspector of the Petersburg District.

Violently swearing at the fool and frightened himself, Lieutenant Koshkul 2nd broke off the interrogation, placed the woman under arrest, and drove off in his sleigh with the youth to question him in detail at the police station.

Young Vitushishnikov, who resided on the 22nd Line of Vasilievsky Island, age fifteen, son of a Collegial Registrar, testified that, being a child, he was making his way to the Fishermen's Street in the Petersburg District where, as he heard, a merry-go-round had been set up on the corner of Vvedenye, and children were given a ride for a fee.

Brought up by his father from his earliest years in the spirit of liveliest reverence for the entire August Family, and having a colored portrait always on his wall, he—as he was crossing the above-mentioned spot, observing a certain congregation of people, and realizing what was happening—immediately recognized the Crowned Personage, and, approaching him, placed himself at his disposal. Further, as he came to the city guard's box, he found the guard in a badly enfeebled condition, tottering on his feet and rambling in his speech, who explained to him that he had just dispatched the relief man, either for "swill" or for pills, which he duly reported.

"I must say, you thought fast," the Lieutenant said with respect. "I shall commend you to the Chief of Police as a young man personally known in the most favorable light to the Emperor himself. And now, I have the honor of wishing you a good day. Kindly convey my respects to your esteemed parent. Do not trouble yourself, you will be driven to your domicile in the official sleigh."

17.

If the soldiers had for a moment imagined that it was the Emperor who had stopped at the door of the drinking establishment, they would unquestionably have lost their heads and have been done for. They were saved, and the tavern-keeper ruined, solely through lack of imagination. At the sign of the helmet's peak, the first soldier instantly thought of the local police inspector, and all the subsequent actions in the tavern flowed precisely from this premise and were dictated by the wish to escape from the police, and nothing more.

But even that was sufficient. For a moment both of them felt on their backs the fiery itch of future, and partly of past, blows with a stick. While the calls for the city guards rang in the street, both of them tore away from their seats and rushed, with heads lowered, to the back room, which was the private domain of the tavern-keeper. From there, using the rear door, they ran past the cellar and the privy, and down the narrow stairway into the yard.

The rear of the tavern faced a vacant lot, and there was, properly speaking, no fenced-in yard. There was a fence on one flank only. The boundary of the backyard was marked by potato peels, egg shells, ashes and slops. Therefore, while all the talk went on outside, the soldiers passed without hindrance, with bowed heads, concealing themselves according to the rules of military maneuvers, losing no time and making no noise, to a spot quite a distance away. There they turned off into an alley, deliberately circled this way and that for a while, and then, reaching another district, they separated and went off with a steady, purposeful stride each on his own errand. And to the end of their lives they preserved the memory of how cleverly they got away from the police inspector.

As for the Emperor, what confused him were the unfamiliar conditions of the terrain. The interior of the drinking establishment was covered with dark marbled wallpaper, which, moreover, was spotted by an abundant outcropping of mold. The wallpaper had cracked with age in various places and directions. Therefore the small door in the partition that divided the tavern-keeper's back room from the public area escaped the Emperor's attention.

18.

The horse was lathered. The Emperor was silent all the way back, not responding to bows, with a resolute air. That the soldiers who had entered the tavern vanished as if swallowed up by the earth did not trouble him in the least. He disliked insoluble questions, attributing them to the will of Providence.

If he had found the soldiers, it would have put fear into many hearts, and later might even have become a legend. Then, recounted in appropriate style, it would have occupied its due place. However, in pursuing the soldiers, he had not caught them. And this offended him.

"I'll show them," he repeated over and over.

It was only after he strode through several palace halls, past a series of marble columns, Labrador wood tables, china vases embellished with pictures, and porphyry wares, that the Emperor regained some calm in the easy atmosphere of the palace and returned to the initial point.

Adjutant-General Kleinmichel was summoned.

"Come over, come here, my good man," said the Emperor.

The Adjutant-General hesitated in the doorway.

"Well, what is it, come over," the Emperor said quietly. When he approached, Adjutant-General Kleinmichel was suddenly pinched. He was caught unawares so nimbly and smartly, that he had no time to make a move, either forward or back, and he left his hand at the Emperor's disposal without the least objection.

It was only when the usual nausea attacked that the Emperor released the General and said:

"That, for the curb posts."

On the whole, the high spirits lost in the course of the day were restored. It was clear that the Emperor had reached a decision. After dinner he sent out the telegraph officer on duty and personally dispatched a telegram to the Chief of Gendarmerie Orlov, without address or signature:

"Pig."

It was to this telegram that some historians attributed the cause and origin of the illness that ultimately carried Count Orlov to his grave. As we know, in his old age the Count began to imagine himself a pig, which was first revealed at a state dinner in honor of Count Muraviev, when he suddenly demanded a trough, refusing to eat without it. But this was still in the future.

By evening the Emperor reached an entirely definite decision.

"I'll show them," he said.

He summoned the Chief Superintendent of Police Kokoshkin for a confidential report, and inquired about the results of the investigations. The search, as he expected, remained fruitless. Then, just before evening prayer, the Emperor inscribed his resolution on the report:

"The concessionaire[7] who owns the tavern to be brought to trial. His concession to be annulled. And in case of involvement, his property to be confiscated and turned over to the Treasury."

"I'll show them," he said, "that Autocracy is still alive in Russia."

19.

The tavern turned out to belong to the concessionaire and vintner Konaki, who resided on Bolshaya Morskaya Street. The next day he was arrested on charges of malicious maintenance of taverns owned personally by him. Konaki was not an important figure and quite a recent one. It was only three years since he had arrived from the south, where he owned a large wine cellar. He was a wine merchant from his earliest years, being a hereditary vintner. He knew how to press grapes, what to add to them, and understood the fermentation process. He traded on a large scale. As he paced his cool winery in the south, he enjoyed the taste of prosperity. But his irresistibly growing fortune tore him from these peaceful reflections. He had come to Petersburg to look around, gradually struck roots there, and settled with his large and noisy family on Bolshaya Morskaya. He was already entering into the taste of operations—and now, in broad daylight, unexpectedly, he found himself in a hole.

Actually, not quite unexpectedly. Having in his young sons capable agents in organizing the activities of his drinking establishments, he had learned within two hours about the closing of the tavern. He had estimated the approximate significance of the event and managed to consult several people. Nevertheless, he could not foresee such a lightning-quick loss of freedom. As soon as the door closed on the gendarmes leading away their father, who had lost all his presence of mind, the Konaki sons left the women wailing and rushing about the spacious rooms, and proceeded at once to Konnogvardeisky Boulevard, to see the St. Petersburg concessionaire Rodokanaki.

20.

If Konaki was still a novice, still imbued with the spirit of the Rhenish cellar, Rodokanaki's origins were far behind and forgotten by everyone. All that was known was that he had come from Odessa and, indeed, he himself was always fond of stressing it.

One day he had come to Petersburg, a short man in a black frock coat and a turned-down collar, and bought a plot of land just across from the cavalry barracks, which was an audacity for a civilian. Inviting a prominent architect, he ordered plans and sketches of a house that would be unlike any other in Petersburg, but like all the luxurious southern homes, as in Italy.

"I am a merchant," he explained.

For the gates, he ordered two clay Moorish heads, black, with white teeth and eyes. He had the windows wreathed with ivy, and moved in. The ivy soon dried up, but Rodokanaki became a powerful force in the wine business. If he had tried to merge with the surrounding Petersburg population and with well-born persons in his way of life, his house, and his tastes, everyone would have said of him that he was a Greek, or even, perhaps, a "Grekos." But now everyone paid him visits and spoke of him as an important foreign merchant. And he was fully a member of Petersburg society.

He openly expressed his preference for Odessa, its streets, buildings, and the Grain Exchange, and even set the Odessa almanacs as examples, superior to those of Petersburg.

He had his own tastes.

He paneled the walls with ebony. Everywhere he had ebony, mahogany and walnut. He detested marble.

"This is my home," he would say. "If I want marble, I'll go to the Economic Club and ask the lackey for a menu."

At the Economic Club, of which he was elected steward, he occasionally played cards with famous writers, and he respected those who bested him in the game:

"With such a hand! That's a man for you."

Pushkin, according to him, was puffed up by too much publicity.

He especially disliked *Yevgeny Onegin*, which contained these lines about Odessa:

> "In dusty Odessa . . .
> In dirty Odessa . . .
> I said . . .
> I wanted to say . . . "

"What kind of a poem is that?" he would say.

But generally he did not shun poetry. He tended to admire Benedictov:

> "Behold, this beauteous woman's
> Enchanting bosom."

"That's a picture," he said approvingly.

He also liked this poet's description of a Gypsy camp and of the famous Matryona, whom he had personally heard at Ilya's.

> "And here, in 'The Dark Wood,'
> Matryona is thrashing,
> She thrashes and threshes, she
> seethes and she crushes,

She seethes and she thrashes, she
crushes and threshes,
And now she rises, she soars and
she shakes."

"'Shakes'—that's a picture," he said.

And he added, about the poet:

"Even the old Minister of Finance Kankrin considered him a very able man."

What pleased him most was what he called the poet's *orderliness*, which he found in these lines.

"First he says 'thrashes and threshes, seethes and crushes,' without any order, and then, in proper order: 'She seethes and she thrashes, she crushes and threshes.' That's a man for you."

He liked the bold gesture, the sweeping act, although he himself was a reserved man.

Thus, for example, he admired Jeannette of the Artificial Mineral Waters who had been the first to introduce a separate tax on each hand and each foot.

"That's a woman," he said.

But he was prepared to accept the existence of others as well.

When someone said at this point that the late actress Asenkova had been a saint, Rodokanaki agreed:

"That's something else. She was a saint."

Despite the vast operations he engaged in, he was not in any way an abstract man. He had a lively understanding of people, and the notion of "human frailty" did not exist for him. Everything was only "a matter of habit."

He devised his combinations at night.

On his bedside table he always kept dried gray malaga grapes, cigars, and wine. He pondered his plans, chewed the malaga, washing it down with red wine (good for digestion), smoked a cigar, and fell fast asleep.

When the Konaki sons, connected with him in business matters, came to see him, he told them first of all to calm the women:

"Tell them to stop crying and stay home."

Then, inquiring into the details, he took some notes and let them go, reassured.

He still had not a single idea in his head.

At night, he chewed a twig of malaga, drank a glass of wine, and smoked a cigar.

He composed a preliminary plan of action, and fell asleep.

21.

The next day it became known that Rodokanaki was giving a fashionable ball, at which the great diva, Mme. Schutz herself, would sing.

Rodokanaki usually based his combinations on the habits of the necessary people. If there was a need for a given personage, with certain habits, that personage was invited to honor a dinner with his presence.

No marble, no full-dress uniforms—open, domestic access to a man. The conversation revolved about Karlsbad, Taglioni, Jeannette of the Mineral Waters, the building of a new church or riding school by the architect Thon, about the large losses of Baron Firks at the Economic Club, the giant strides of science in galvanoplastics—all this, depending on the habits of the personage. And, finally, about Vaudeville-Cañones cigars.

"I like Trabucco," Rodokanaki would say.

If the guest also liked Trabucco, a footman delivered two boxes of the finest to him the very next day.

The entire conversation was conducted in subdued tones. Rodokanaki was attentive and treated even the question of Jeannette with all seriousness. The Minister of Finance was interested in her destiny, and the choice of subject at the table expressed, as it were, a high regard for the guest. In the matter of wine concessions Rodokanaki was considered the strongest dialectician. He never allowed the footman to interrupt him with urgent business.

"I am not home," he would say coldly and without turning.

And it was only as the guest was about to leave that the necessary topics were broached, and if the conditions set by the interested parties were acceptable, everything was settled. If not, there was further search, new acquaintances, complex maneuvers, and another, more important, and above all, more tractable personage was found.

All of this took place in the presence of solid wooden walls, parquet floors, antique rugs and collections of Chinese bronzes, and proceeded in a calm and profoundly thorough, even historic manner. And, indeed, every object here had its own history—the beer tankard on the fireplace was a gift from Prince Bouter in Karlsbad, the bronzes were from China.

"A great merchant," the charmed personage would comment with a sigh.

This was when the question at hand concerned some single, clear-cut matter.

But when the matter was diffuse or even elusive in its sphere of action, when it was necessary first to select the persons, to feel out their habits and catch the moral tenor of the day, there was a reception, a ball. Principal attention was paid to the ladies, and in this there were simple reliable combinations. At such times a variety of commissions and committees were formed and dissolved all at once, new people emerged, and the ladies served as the mutual ground and object, unifying the most diverse agencies which had lost their common language, and prompting even the highest official personages to adopt a light, bantering tone.

This time the invitations were issued to the most important dealers in the wine business, one young man from Justice, one personage from Finance, several other men's wives, men of letters, and cartoonists.

22.

Outwardly, the ball was a success. There was no stiffness, merely full attention to rank and merits. Footmen carried trays of lemonade and soda water. The guests were served *poularde à la Napolitaine,* grouse *en papillote*, eggs *à la* Baron Velkersamm. Rodokanaki had an excellent chef. Every dish had its own history: the oysters came from Ostende, the wines from Les Pres.

Madame Rodokanaki, middle-aged, in a voile dress, who usually sequestered herself in the inner rooms, sat near the mahogany sideboard, in the role of hostess.

The wine and spirits business was represented by Utkin, in a black evening coat, Likharev, and Baron Fitinghof (a front). Utkin was a master dodger, a man who could outwit anyone, but his vanity led him into embarrassing positions: he entertained literary pretensions. He had subsidized an illustrated journal, and suddenly it appeared with a caricature on himself. Likharev was a man of the Moscow school, in a long-waisted Russian coat, with a smiling face and hair cut straight across the nape and forehead. Baron Fitinghof was a false front in tightly fitting trousers.

The diva, Mme. Schutz, sang a roulade from *Idol Mio* and left at once, with her fee in an envelope.

A poet-journalist recited a poem about the latest dance:

> "Faster, faster, quick allegro!
> Dance owes no obedience to fate!
> Gentlemen, as black as negroes,
> Catch the ladies, butterflies of May!"

Another man's wife slapped him on the wrist with her fan.

"Ah, how Matryona flung down her hat: 'Ulane, Ulane!'"

"Live a while in our Petersburg, Cleopatra Ivanovna, watch every hour add refinement to refinement."

"Tom Pouce is a midget, that's true, but he is also a general. He was awarded the rank of general. Oh, yes! Last year."

"And so she comes over to me, and in Karlsbad all the girls wear uniform caps and white formal jackets—they're strict about it there."

"He rings a bell and eats with a fork. If you ask how old he is, he barks three times. He writes his name, Emile, and walks off on his hind legs."

"She said to him, 'Your Excellency, you may not like my voice, but you must admire my charms.'"

"Now silk for the ladies will be made from hemp. They're already selling shares."

"That's something else. It's special hemp."

Yet Rodokanaki was troubled.

Some people did not come. There were too many other men's wives and poets. Jeannette from the Artificial Mineral Waters, from whom he had expected much because of her special closeness with the Finance Minister, was away on tour. The man from Justice sent an apology, and the Privy Councillor from Finance exuded such cold and fog that the rest, from the various committees, were suddenly overcome with the sense of their official positions. The famed cozy atmosphere of the Rodokanaki evenings seemed to have changed. The style was gone. One lady, with a stout rear, was positively too free and easy. The writers drank too much. There was an undercurrent of chill and emptiness, and—the tested barometer—Panteleyev, of the commissions, looked about him too absently and sourly.

The important guests departed earlier than usual.

Then, leaving the other men's wives and the cartoonists to finish off the *poulardes*, Rodokanaki quietly slipped away to his study with the wine merchants—Utkin, Likharev, and Baron Fitinghof (a front).

His last words that evening were as follows:

"Whether Konaki lives or not does not concern me. One Greek more or less. But an arrest—an arrest is something else."

23.

The next morning the Minister of Finance, Privy Councillor Vronchenko, received the Commercial Councillor Rodokanaki.

The Minister was a portly man. Accepting him into the Service, the former Minister Kankrin judged that "he would not invent gunpowder." The time had come when precisely such Ministers were needed. It was also said of him that he was "strong on hindsight." That too proved useful. When he became Minister, Vronchenko displayed excellent masculine qualities and wit. His sayings gained wide currency. For example, when the Minister agreed to something, he would say "It be." If not, the reply was "Not be." And, he would take a pinch of snuff.

It was said that he was paraphrasing Hamlet's famous phrase, "To be or not to be."

In general, he was in every way a statesman, who personally understood the full importance of finances.

He received Rodokanaki coolly but politely.

"Come in, please, sit down, here, on the sofa."

Rodokanaki stated the purpose of his visit and expressed his wish that the tavern-keeper be punished with utmost severity, and Konaki be released, if possible.

Minister Vronchenko did not agree and even frowned.

"His own fault. *Il est coupable.*"

Rodokanaki said that persons who perform mercantile functions cannot be held responsible for persons who visit drinking establishments, and that Utkin, Likharev, and Baron Fitinghof hoped that Konaki would not be brought to trial.

"That be," said the Minister and sniffed a pinch of tobacco with an indifferent air.

At that point Commercial Councillor Rodokanaki sighed, and added that he was not speaking in his own name. His position was quite another matter. He had long been ready for retirement, and the trading operations had become too arduous for him. However, he was obliged to convey to His Excellency in the name of the above-mentioned persons, and, well, his own too, that all of them were planning to establish a joint stock company for silk production. They would therefore no longer be able to carry the concessions and were compelled to withdraw from them.

"Not be?" said the astonished Vronchenko and fairly jumped up in his seat.

"With deep regrets, Your Excellency, it be," Rodokonaki said with a rueful smile, bowing out.

24.

It was only after Rodokonaki's departure that Vronchenko recollected himself.

"What the devil? *Il est fou.* Has he gone mad?" he said to his secretary, who happened to come by. "What the devil is all that about silk?"

But he soon realized that silk had a purely nominal significance in the entire affair, and remembered that the wine concessions brought in twenty million. And that all the special revenues, in toto and in round figures, came approximately, God willing, to forty. As for extra expenditures, they were entirely unpredictable and unavoidable.

Finance Minister Vronchenko was overcome with a sense of loneliness. He asked himself what the great Kankrin would have done in his place, and even shaded his eyes with his hand, emulating his predecessor, who, suffering from weak eyesight, always pulled a green visor over his forehead during office hours to protect his eyes from light.

Finding no answer, Vornchenko turned to his secretary with a phrase in which he summed up the situation:

"Everything considered . . . "

There was no reply.

Puffing up his cheeks and blowing out a few times, he caught his breath and decided that changes were possible.

He resolved to see some colleagues in the Ministries, and to undertake nothing personally until evening.

25.

A man distraught will court inevitable failure. Vronchenko's first visit was to the Minister of Justice, Panin.

The Minister was noted for his bluntness. Interpreting the principle of unbending probity in its literal sense, he did not bow his head before anyone save his Sovereign. If he happened to drop his handkerchief or his spectacles, tall as he was, he lowered himself on his haunches to pick them up, never bending his back. He was known for his high moral standards, exaggerated rumors of which reached even foreign courts.

Explaining the gist of the matter to Panin, Vronchenko pointed out that, actually, *entre nous deux,* a tavern-owner cannot keep track of everyone and be responsible for everyone, and asked for help.

"For we're in trouble."

Panin replied frankly:

"I am always glad, my dear Fyodor Pavlovich, to hear your arguments when they concern justice. I assure you that the culprits will be severely punished. A crime such as you describe cannot remain unpunished in an enlightened country. But I shall make every effort to safeguard the peace of your Ministry."

Taking a pinch of snuff, he proceeded to Levashov, but the General was engaged in his morning calisthenics, as could be heard from his room.

"One! Two! Heave!"

Making his way, on his weary horse, to Alexey Fyodorovich Orlov, Vronchenko wilted, sagged, noted that the weather had changed. The snow was thawing, his sideburns were wet, he felt as if he had never been a minister at all.

Alexey Fyodorovich Orlov greeted him, with his usual military stance.

His first words were brisk, full of energy:

"Sit down! What is it?"

But after Vronchenko's second sentence he became altogether abstracted, kept examining his heels, twisting the ends of his shoulder-knot into curlicues, and finally, with a peculiar, piglike, grunt, he said:

"Sure enough, I know that finances are needed, but going to taverns is strictly forbidden."

Emerging into the street and finding complete slush and muddy melting snow, Vronchenko glanced up at the orphaned blue and, saying to himself, "Into retirement!" he ordered the coachman:

"Drive home."

26.

During his next report to the Sovereign, Vronchenko fought to screw up his courage and finally, turning purple, he declared that things were in bad shape with the concessions.

He had been struggling for a long time to prepare himself for this report.

The Emperor interrupted him.

"Wipe your nose," he said sternly.

This could have been understood literally, for it was true that at times of extreme anxiety the Minister was wont to take a great deal of snuff, so that his later supposition that "a drop hung from his nose" at that moment may have had a foundation in fact. The Emperor had a hereditary revulsion to tobacco. But, on the other hand, it could have been understood as a command to resign.

Immediately after this report it became known that the Minister of Finance was about to retire within a day or two.

27.

When Count Kleinmichel heard that Vronchenko was in trouble with the concessions, his spirits rose.

"The swine," he said. "Let him sit without millions for a while, the swine. Anyone can manage with millions."

And when the rumor spread that Vronchenko was resigning, he became altogether merry.

"He is going into retirement," he said to the Director of the Department of Public Buildings. "Fine, let him go, the swine."

The Director also expressed his satisfaction, but added that there were likely to be changes now in the balance and the budget.

"What changes? Why?"

The Director explained that loss of the concessions would mean a difference of some twenty-odd million for the Finance Administration.

"Of course, it would. Let him sit without millions, the swine," the Count said, but suddenly it came to him that the swine was retiring, while he, the Count, remained.

He talked things over with a few people.

By evening he sank into deep thought and rapidly began to pace his study.

A bottle of seltzer was placed on his desk by the solicitous Countess, as always on such occasions.

It suddenly became clear to him that, with millions gone, there would be no money for building railways and bridges. And with no money for building, they would not be built. That meant the disappearance, to begin with, of contractors.

Count Kleinmichel saw an abyss of ruin opening before him.

28.

The rumors which spread instantly and all at once were of a particularly malicious character.

It was whispered in the ear and with a wary glance over the shoulder that two soldiers threatened the life of the Emperor, but that he had been saved by a young stripling. Others, chiefly from among the military, retorted irritably that, on the contrary, the impudent young scamp threw a snowball at the Emperor, but was arrested by a police lieutenant and was currently held in the Fortress of Peter and Paul.

The retirement of the Finance Minister received wide publicity, although it had not yet been announced. The cause, according to general opinion was the scandalous Jeannette of the Artificial Mineral Waters.

In the reports of the French attaché Fontenelle to his government, the affair was described more precisely: A group of prominent concessionaires, something similar to the *fermiers généraux* of the old regime, *d'ancien régime,* in France, had put forth a claim on the government for fifty million rubles; the population is in panic; the Finance Minister was removed from his post and is spending his days with the notorious Jeannette on Meshchanskaya Street. An attempt on the Emperor's life was made during a hunting trip (*oblava russe*).

The attaché wrote, *Aut nunc aut nunquam*—now or never.

29.

He sat with his family. The sense of domestic happiness took the place of all others. On such days he required that a real samovar be brought to the tea table and that the Empress herself pour the tea. He jested continuously with the young Maids-in-Waiting and related a historic incident from his youth, when the chevalier who was his tutor assigned him the following topic for a composition:

"Military service is not the only service for a nobleman; there are other occupations as well." After an hour and a half, the Emperor, who was in his fiifteenth year, handed his tutor a blank sheet of paper. The shoulders of the Maids-in-Waiting twitched at this story.

Neither at the tea, nor at any time, was there any mention of Varenka Nelidova.

Nevertheless, his state of mind could not be termed serene. The Emperor, in addition to all else, was endowed with a powerful, if aging, nature, which demanded its exercise. This could be seen in his face as well, which one courtier compared to the harp of Aeolus, as it reflected every mood of the elements.

In state matters, however, he was adamant. Kleinmichel, who ventured in his report on the bridge to introduce the expression "financial estimate," was simply thrown out.

The afternoon nap was followed by a small game of whist at low stakes: the Emperor never played for more than twenty-five kopeks a point. Three chamberlains were invited to the game—two young ones, and one old. Beckoning to one of the little Maids-in-Waiting, who blushed down to her bosom, he appointed her his advisor.

The Maid-in-Waiting, prettily animated, diligently offered advice, and the Emperor did as he saw fit. Thus, despite her advice, he chose to start with an ace, which, as everyone knows, is wrong in whist in the presence of an ace, a king, and three low cards.

"Your Majesty," said the blissful but frightened young woman, "but no one does that!"

The Emperor replied with unexpected asperity:

"I do."

"Your Majesty," the Maid-in-Waiting mumbled, "but the usual system in whist. . . . "

The Emperor put down the ace.

"*Le système Nicolas*," he said.

The young chamberlain visibly turned pale and took a long time in selecting a card. At last he chose, put it down—and lost.

"*Le système Nicolas*," repeated the Emperor.

The second rubber began. The players changed places, so that each would have the opportunity to partner the Emperor.

The old chamberlain was in his eighties. He was deaf and noticed nothing around him, not even women's eyes. He was absorbed in the game.

"*Le système* . . . " The Emperor began.

Within a single minute, the chamberlain covered all of the Emperor's cards with his trembling hands.

The Emperor put on the table the three rubles he lost, and turned his back on the players.

"I am not rich enough for card games," he said, exhibiting a dour smile under his moustache. "To be ignored," he added unexpectedly, with a stern glance at all the players, and walked out of the room, with his chest high.

The domestic circle broke up. The old chamberlain was never again invited to court.

In the evening of the same day, news came of shaky rates at the London Exchange.

30.

Two students, suspiciously silent, were seen on Vasilievsky Island, not far from the site of the incident.

A townsman on Kuznetsky Bridge was proposing to "Let the rooster fly—put a match to it all."

The three were arrested.

Faddey Venedictovich Bulgarin had unexpected visitors in his solitary retirement.

He was no longer the learned man of letters, bursting with vitality and activity, whom Petersburg had known in former times. But even now he lived in unceasing labors. Just recently, he had obtained the post of corresponding member of the Special Commission on Horse-Breeding, and, in connection with this new employment, began to publish a journal, *The Steward*.

"Horses, horses are my passion," he said.

For his lifelong labors he was awarded the rank of Active Councillor of State.

Among his major works, he had prepared for publication *A Winner From Dinner, Sketches of XVIIth Century Manners and Morals*, and began to print it at his own expense, illustrated with wood engravings.

In the summer he lived in the country, and in winter, in his spacious Petersburg apartment, where —vying with Grech[8]—he installed a huge cage, taking up half a room, in which he kept songbirds. Every spring he opened a window and released one of the birds, reciting as he did a verse of the late Pushkin:

> "I let a captive bird go free."

This event drew to the street a large crowd of urchins, street vendors, and neighbors, who knew that the writer Bulgarin annually set free one of his birds.

He was pondering the plan of his memoirs. In speaking with young writers, he declared that there was essentially no difference between him and Pushkin.

"We both had always tried to be useful to our superiors."

And he added:

"Except that one was successful, and the other got a fig."

And finally, leaning confidentially toward the listener, he whispered in his ear:

"Actually, he was an empty vessel."

Now Faddey Venedictovich received visitors in connection with an important matter.

There were three of them: a Colonel of the Special Corps of the Gendarmerie, Lieutenant Koshkul 2nd, and a civilian personage.

They requested and expected his aid as the editor of *The Northern Bee*, in order to calm the people's minds.

Faddey Venedictovich asked Lieutenant Koshkul 2nd to describe the entire incident in detail, and sat down, pen in hand, to think. All three followed with respect the changes of expression on his face, fully understanding that this was inspiration.

Faddey Venedictovich batted his eyes. The eyes, behind large spectacles, had no eyelashes.

He began to think out loud:

"We can put it that two mad dogs attacked, and the youth courageously. . . . No, it won't do."

"We can also have two wolves running in from nearby villages. . . . Wolves—that's very suitable, romantic. But the youth. . . . No, it won't do. . . . "

Everything appeared unsuitable, and would not do for the simple reason that the Emperor was a model in all things. Thus, for example, the story of two mad dogs and a youth bravely fighting them off might have been fine, but would not do: if they attacked the Emperor himself, they surely would have bitten others.

The story of the wolves from nearby villages was romantic, but inconsistent with street traffic. Replacing the wolves with foxes would render the youth's intervention absurd.

Suddenly, his eyes narrowed, and Faddey Venedictovich turned to Lieutenant Koshkul 2nd.

"Now, my dear sir, if you please," he said to the Lieutenant. "Would you sketch for me the ground plan of the incident? On this scrap of paper."

Lieutenant Koshkul 2nd indicated the vacant lot, the sentry box, the tavern, and the Emperor's sleigh.

"The river, please," Faddey Venedictovich said impatiently.

The Lieutenant traced the line of the river on the side.

Then Faddey Venedictovich drew a circle beyond the line, and, with a flourish, planted a dot within the circle, and wrote "W."

"A woman," he explained to the nonplussed Lieutenant Koshkul 2nd. "Drowning. In an ice-hole."

31

The very next day *The Northern Bee* carried in its section on The People's Ways an article entitled "The Wonder-Child, or the Rescue of a Drowning Victim, Rewarded by the Monarch."

"On the outskirts of town," the article related, "a young peasant girl daily drew water from an ice-hole in the Large Nevka River. Suddenly—cr-rash! The thin ice gave way under her feet. The unfortunate girl, seeing no one to rescue her, sank into the water. From time to time she emitted a long scream and looked with tears into the open sky. But Providence! . . . She hears a voice above her—someone hastens to help. It is the young Mr. Vitushish3-nikov, who resides on the 22nd Line of Vasilievsky Island with his aged father, Collegial Registrar Vitushishnikov. Being a mere child, he was hastening to the Petersburg District for childish games. But, hearing the piteous cries and following the dictates of his heart, he turned to aid the drowning girl. However, the immature arms of the youth were unable to sustain the victim. It seemed that both the girl and her youthful rescuer were equally exhausted. But the Monarch, as he was driving by on his tireless labors for the people's weal, heard the cries of innocence. And, like his glorious forebear,[9] he extended the mantle of aid. . . .

"Soon the rescued pair was warming up in the box of the city guards, and their lives have now been declared out of danger. Providence! . . .

"In honor of this Historic Day, a Memorial Board will be nailed without delay on the wall of the sentry box to keep the memory alive for distant posterity.

"The editors, in their close concern with the future of the wonder-child, hereby announce the collection of voluntary contributions for the purchase of a home for him. Mr. Lieutenant Koshkul 2nd has offered to serve as the organizer of his fortune and will take charge of the collection at the office of the newspaper *The Northern Bee.*

"The following persons have agreed to contribute to the philanthropic collection: the Right Honorable Mr. Alyakrinsky—3 silver rubles; the Right Honorable Mr. Bulgarin—1 silver ruble; The Honorable Mr. Lieutenant Koshkul 2nd—1 silver ruble; Commercial Councillor Rodokanaki—200 silver rubles.

Subscriptions are also accepted for the deluxe edition, with 100 illustrations, of the historical novel, *A Winner From Dinner. Sketches of XVIIth Century Manners and Morals,* by Mr. F. V. Bulgarin. "

32.

And yet serenity did not come.

The Emperor heard the name Rodokanaki. This was a new name; he had not heard it before. The Emperor asked his Marshal, de Ribeaupierre. Always candid, Ribeaupierre responded with honest puzzlement. He knew only two similar names—Rodofinikin and Rode;[10] the latter belonged to a musician, therefore he omitted mentioning it. None of the chamberlains knew Rodokanaki or wished to admit it. By the sound of it, however, the name must have been Greek.

The Greek Ambassador, a friend of Ribeaupierre, was a German, spoke German, was born in Bavaria, was in high favor with King Otto,[11] and was generally unfamiliar with Greek names.

With a frigid expression, the Emperor suddenly asked Kleinmichel during his report:

"What is Rodokanaki?"

It seemed to Count Kleinmichel that he was suspected of something.

"I do not know, Your Majesty."

"But I know," said the Sovereign.

Kleinmichel paled. However, the Emperor actually did not know who, or, as he said, what Rodokanaki was.

Toward evening he finally obtained an answer. Rodokanaki turned out to be an altogether private individual, a concessionaire who had the temerity to reside across from the cavalry barracks. With a secret shudder, the Emperor repeated:

"Rodokanaki!"

He resolved to take extreme measures.

33.

The Minister of the Court was summoned. The Emperor asked for the schedule of expenditures. He glanced at it, was displeased, and sighed.

"I cannot spend so much money. Take away this paper."

He demanded reduction in the number of candles in the chandeliers to two in each, which made for an economy in candles throughout the palace. He sent for the daily dinner menus, and crossed out the *blanc-manger* with his own hand.

"I insist, do you hear, insist—there must be no debt in the state," he said, with a hard stern look at the Minister.

A hush descended on the palace.

Coming into the Apollo Hall, the Emperor suddenly ordered the removal of the statue of Silenus.

"A drunken Greek," he said.

In the evening an ancient utterance[12] was heard, which made people turn pale:

"*Le sang coulera!* There will be blood."

34.

Rodokanaki had acted in the hope that matters would soon be resolved. He had no intention whatever to discontinue his concessions. Retaining all his habits and outward calm, Rodokanaki was inwardly troubled and even lost a game at the Economic Club. The worst of the situation was that he was bound in his actions with other persons. Utkin was unreliable, in Rodokanaki's opinion, ready to sell out at any moment. Likharev had grown silent. Baron Fitinghof (a false front) was too talkative.

All this expressed itself even in the fact that all of them, not excepting Rodokanaki himself, began, as if in concert, to add abusive epithets to Konaki's name.

"When that numbskull Konaki was still free. . . . "

"That blockhead Konaki might have thought of. . . . "

"Remember, at the club, when that dolt Konaki gorged himself on sturgeon. . . . "

Their sacrifice, for such a wretched individual, began to seem to them ridiculous, stupid, and totally inappropriate. And, saying nothing to one another for the time being, they told their wives, or even other men's wives:

"Got into this mess with the scoundrel Konaki. . . . "

They even exaggerated their sacrifice, since their customary operations had not been discontinued, and there had been only spoken and, in part, written actions, although admittedly quite far-reaching. Besides, the fluctuations on the Exchange had for a time engaged their full energies and attention. They had all banked on a decline, and even Konaki gave instructions to his sons from prison as to which notes were to be sold.

All the wine and spirits dealers unprotestingly sent their contributions to *The Northern Bee*.

Rodokanaki said in this regard:

"This is something else. This is a child."

At night he chewed malaga.

He was devising combinations.

Meantime, Minister Vronchenko, though he had not taken refuge in the brothel on Meshchanskaya Street, as was falsely reported by the French agent, was at any rate actually devoting all his free time and attention to Jeannette of the Artificial Mineral Waters, who had meantime returned from her tour and resumed her usual duties.

Having received no exact instructions after the historic phrase, and, on the other hand, seeing that the concessionaires refused to accept the removal of Konaki, Privy Councillor Vronchenko seemed to be suspended in mid-air, and watched with dull indifference the fluctuations of the Exchange.

The Finance Ministry was, so to speak, performing its natural daily functions purely mechanically, without inspiration. Officials came and went, committees met, but the spirit had flown.

During this period of disarray, Lieutenant Koshkul 2nd was deep in feverish activity. The subscription toward the purchase of a home for the wonder-child proceeded successfully. His honor Mendt, von, contributed 1 silver ruble; the mother of a family, Mme. N. — 1 silver ruble; Second Guild Merchant Myakin — 10 silver rubles.

35.

And the youth's fortune was arranged.

A little house was found on Krestovsky Island and purchased from the woman who owned it. An artist was called in, who decorated the roof with lace-like carvings and skillfully painted flower-pots and sheaves on the shutters. The result was a little house which might have been designed by nature itself for an invalid who had grown old in the Tsar's service and was now modestly devoted to bringing up his son. With the remaining money, Lieutenant Koshkul 2nd bought for young Mr. Vitushishnikov a drum, so that the child might learn to play it in his spare time. The drum was an excellent one, with a bright and piercing tone. All this was reported to the subscribers and readers of *The Northern Bee* in the department of "St. Petersburg Events."

The greatest trouble was with the father, Collegial Registrar Vitushishnikov. To begin with, he did not turn out to be as aged as had been supposed. Secondly, he objected to being moved to Krestovsky Island, where he was thenceforth to dedicate himself to the duties of fatherhood.

He cited such arguments as that Krestovsky Island was too far from his place of employment, that he had lived on Vasilievsky Island for seventeen years, and so on. Lieutenant Koshkul 2nd was even obliged to raise his voice with him. On the other hand, the Lieutenant tempted him with the chicken-coop next to the house, where he would be able to keep chickens.

After the move, young Vitushishnikov learned to drum a lively reveille. And it was promptly decided to place him in one of the closed military schools.

Next came the episode related by a military historian:

The young grand duchesses, out for a drive, quite accidentally passed by the little house where young Mr. Vitushishnikov resided with his aged invalid-father. The youth stood at the gate, dressed in the uniform of the military school. At the sight of the duchesses, he struck up a brisk tattoo on his drum. His invalid-father, who was standing next to him, stepped forward, offering the royal duchesses the traditional welcome of bread and salt, served on a simple platter covered with a clean lace-trimmed towel.

Neither was the sentry-box of the city guard forgotten. A plain white marble plaque was installed on it, just above the window, stating in golden letters that "The Emperor Nicholas I graciously honored this booth with his presence on the 12th day of February, 184 . . . , and observed the warming up of a woman newly saved from drowning."

36.

Count Kleinmichel was in a state of decline. Thrown out by the Emperor for the words "financial estimate," unpardonably remiss in answering the question about Rodokanaki, he was visibly sagging. With difficulty he had to force himself to shave, and sprouted a reddish bristle. He was treated with poultices and powders for his chest, he suffered constant nausea. Symptoms of hemorrhoids appeared. From time to time the electro-magnetic apparatus recorded faint sounds. In momentary hope that this was the Emperor tapping, the Count rushed to the telegraph room and pushed aside the officer on duty, but the apparatus fell silent. Either the will of the Emperor, or the effect of atmospheric vibrations. In addition, he was also burdened with official duties. The difficult question of railway tenders[13] was under consideration. The Count had always thought that tenders were a special kind of lifeboats, and now he simply did not know what to do with them on land. Yet large sums of money were involved.

The Count's sister, an elderly spinster, who visited her brother and found him in a desperate state, pleaded with him to go to their Lutheran church and pray.

The Count replied that he would not go to any church because Luther was a swine.

"Orthodoxy, Autocracy, and Nationality," he said to the shocked woman. "And Luther was a swine."

37.

The Ministry of the Court combined within its purview the Quarters of the Maids-in-Waiting, the Imperial Academy of the Arts, the Hunt, the Clergy, and the Stables. The Director of the state stud farm, Levashov, spoke in rapid whispers:

"Form, form and form, my dear Sirs! What form! What points! Flanks!"

The Prussian painter Franz Kruge, who was expressly invited from abroad to paint portraits, spoke of the famous mare, Favorite:

"The main thing is the legs. Leanness of the legs is a mark of breed. An oval croup, and arching flanks."

The experienced Kammer-Frau Baranova defined the requisite condition and duties of the Maids-in-Waiting in the following terms:

"Incense. Gothic, Gothic, Gothic. Do you sense the fragrance?"

Kammer-Frau Baranova taught the young Maids-in-Waiting to be hardy. In Peterhof, in the little house of the Empress, which the Empress occasionally visited, it was extremely damp, the walls were dripping. The little house was reminiscent of a small antique temple, but was built on a tiny island in the lake, which had formerly been a swamp.

In this lake stood a plaster statue of a young woman, up to her waist in the water. When one of the Maids-in-Waiting complained of the damp, the Kammer-Frau would take her by the hand and point to the statue:

"Take a lesson from her."

The Emperor decorated the little house with a variety of objects of antique character. Exact copies were made of the lamps found during the excavation of the pagan city of Pompeii, which had been buried in ashes soon after the Birth of Christ. To the general embarrassment, all the lamps turned out to be highly dubious in shape and evoked indescribable comparisons. The Maids-in-Waiting were strictly and forever forbidden to think about it. And, indeed, in their calling, they could not even know anything about the objects of comparison.

Kammer-Frau Baranova explained the lamps to them.

"It's Gothic," she said. "True, it is pagan Gothic, but Gothic all the same."

The temple which the Emperor had ordered to be constructed in Alexandria, his Peterhof summer home, a "baby temple," as people referred to it, was pure Gothic and bore no likeness to pot-bellied cupolas. Pointing to the lancet windows and the stone lace and ruffles in the corners, Kammer-Frau Baranova would say:

"Take a lesson from them."

The Maids-in-Waiting were filled with airy yearnings, and in the mornings they recounted their dreams to one another. They all dreamt of the Emperor in various guises.

The art of tip-toeing, speaking in undertone, and listening attentively they assimilated from the very first days. They were distinguished by delicate sensibility and caught the vaguest allusions. They were possessed by the fantastic. The English writer, Miss Radcliffe[14] was their moral catechism.

"Magnetism, magnetism!" they exclaimed. "Ah, that magnetism!"

From the moment of the Emperor's quarrel with Nelidova everything came into a state of extraordinary agitation. They caught each other in corners with secret, significant handshakes. They exchanged glances. Parties were formed, which waged wars invisible to outsiders. Almost all of them stopped sleeping, almost all dreamt of either the Emperor or Varenka Nelidova. One of the Maids-in-Waiting was visited by the shade of Marie-Antoinette. Another saw in her dream the Emperor Alexander I, who said "This is I," but what he meant remained unclear.

Meantime, Varenka Nelidova who, in her break with the Emperor, exhibited a degree of courage that astonished everyone, lost all presence of mind immediately after the break. The idea of making a personal appearance or tapping out a message on the electro-magnetic apparatus filled her with mortal terror.

38.

In the morning a miracle occurred.

A man of remarkably ordinary appearance, dressed in a short peasant's coat, came and brought an envelope with two hundred thousand rubles in banknotes. The envelope bore the words, "*A M-lle Nelidoff.*" The money was accompanied by a note, "For the orphanage. Commercial Councillor R." Asked whether he had been instructed to convey any verbal message, the bearer begged that prayers be said for those in prison, and departed, leaving everyone stunned.

Where to go, whom to inform, whom to consult about the money?

There still survived some relics of the old generation of Maids-in-Waiting, who knew the era of Marya Savvishna Perekusikhina. But, though incredibly experienced, these veteran ladies were deaf and blind, knew nothing of magnetism, and used murderous Horse-Guard language.

There were still some living Maids-in-Waiting of the preceding reign, which was known among the Maids-in-Waiting as the epoch of *Marie*—after Maria Antonovna Naryshkina. But they were held in total contempt, and, when they occasionally appeared at court, they were so agitated that they pattered with mincing steps like little girls.

Then, already under the new Emperor, there had at first been an era of masquerades, when he sought to merge with the country and descended to ladies of the third estate, and, after that, an era of diversity.

With Kammer-Frau Baranova one could discuss the miracle, but to talk of the money would be inappropriate.

There was no one to consult.

Nelidova went to see Count Kleinmichel. Count Kleinmichel and his wife, Dame Kleinmichel, a relation of Nelidova, were thrown into extreme agitation. The Count trembled, as if subject to the action of electro-magnetic currents.

"Two hundred thousand," he said. "For the indigent young! That is too much for them."

First of all, he asked Nelidova what orphanage the note referred to. But Nelidova knew nothing herself. Then Dame Kleinmichel, examining the lists of all existing orphanages, established that Nelidova was indeed a patroness of a home for indigent children.

Neither the address, nor the dimensions of this institution were indicated. Varenka Nelidova had never visited it.

Count Kleinmichel's advice was to accept the money and make inquiries about the orphanage.

"Accept the money without delay," he said to Nelidova. "And pray for the prisoner."

"What prisoner?" Nelidova asked, shutting her eyes with terror.

"For that . . . " said the Count, "that swine . . . the concessioned. . . . "

And the Count related, quite coherently, that a swine-concessionaire was being held in prison, and that it was essential at any cost to set him free—or everything would be lost. In a hoarse whisper he declared to the deeply moved Varenka Nelidova that she could become the savior of the country, like Joan of Arc.

And the Count made the arrangements.

The address of the home for indigent children was found. The Superintendent of the home was summoned. On that very day the infants labored with mops to eradicate the odor of sour cabbage. A ball was organized in honor of the patroness. In the evening the infants marched quite neatly, across the modest, freshly white-washed hall of the home, stretching their toes, as if on drill. And later, with the aid of the Superintendent, they sang the cantata, "The Heavens Flash and Thunder," and played games.

In the evening calm returned to her.

She fell asleep, recalling the children's marching step and the cantata.

On the following day she visited Dame Kleinmichel. The Count, who was suffering his usual attack, walked in his slippers from morning. Suddenly a clear, sharp sound was heard from the study.

The electro-magnetic apparatus was tapping.

39.

The Emperor's strong nature could no longer endure the strain. He tapped uninterruptedly, demanding the immediate arrival of the Court Maid-in-Waiting Varvara Arkadievna Nelidova. Excuses by reason of illness were rejected in advance.

Count Kleinmichel buttoned himself up from top to bottom before the apparatus and clapped his slippered heels.

"Yes, Your Majesty," he said quietly.

"Lively!" the apparatus indicated.

Coming out to the ladies in a military stride the Count spoke with tears in his eyes, turning to the Maid-in-Waiting Nelidova:

"He is calling."

After Nelidova's departure, the Count's boots had barely been pulled on when the apparatus started again.

"She is on the way," the Count telegraphed, clicking his heels.

"Well done," the Emperor replied, by *le système Nicolas*.

The Count immediately ordered the barber to be called in to shave him.

40.

It sometimes takes a mere ten minutes to resolve the most complex problems of history.

Varenka Nelidova returned to discipline. The simple, even severe character of the Emperor's campaign study lent the reconciliation special weight.

"Pardon," said Varenka Nelidova.

"I do," replied the Emperor.

"The concessionaire," she said suddenly.

Outside, beyond the walls, flowed the life of his capital; here—the life of his heart. Guards Regiments marched along the streets of the capital, swinging their feet forward; symmetrical projects were in progress; bridges were erected across the Neva River by the engineer Colonel D'Estrem. The financial fluctuations were ending. It was possible now to permit *blanc-manger* for tomorrow. At ease, at ease!

41.

People were at a loss to understand the sudden release of the concessionaire Konaki, a native of Vinnitsa, who resided in the house of the merchant Korzukhin on Bolshaya Morskaya Street, and who was accused of tempting soldiers of the Chasseurs Life Guards Regiment to drunkenness.

A historian of the juridical school was uncertain how to explain the fact that it had not occurred to anyone, not even in the Ministry of Justice, that the very existence of a separate room in the tavern was in itself an illegal act, and hence Konaki's imprisonment for the purpose of conducting an investigation was an entirely legitimate act.

The psychological school, in analyzing the Emperor's state of mind, attributed everything to the unpredictable manifestations of his character.

The Vice-Director Ignatov, whom Count Kleinmichel had called a swine and later had in some manner insulted or passed over, left his memoirs, in which he asserted that the Emperor, alarmed at the instability of the Exchange, retreated before Konaki; that the appeal of the Maid-in-Waiting Nelidova was granted so promptly because the Emperor himself had supposedly been waiting impatiently for some way of finally putting an end to the affair.

The facts were much simpler.

To begin with, how could the so-called "swine Ignatov" have known the facts? Besides, if anyone were to be mentioned, it should have been Rodokanaki, and certainly not Konaki. Konaki was an entirely insignificant individual, and was even obliged to postpone reimbursing Rodokanaki for his expenditures in the case for a whole year. But then, Rodokanaki himself was a private person. He did not serve in any official capacity, and for that reason alone, as historians of the juridical school pointed out, could not have had any influence in affairs of state.

He was a merchant, a concessionaire, and that was all.

The true explanation was that the Emperor, as he often did, simply dropped the entire matter.

Finances were abandoned for the time being—
he did not wish to be troubled with them any
longer. The very word was omitted in reports. The
candles were lit, *blanc-manger* was once again served
at the table. He put the entire problem out of his
mind. Vronchenko returned to his duties. Customs
continued as before.

It might be that, deep in his heart, the Emperor
took pity on the imprisoned Konaki and fully con-
tented himself with the exile of the criminal tavern-
mistress to penal labor. Besides, with his chivalrous
understanding of masculine duties, he could not
be false to a promise given to a woman at such a
moment.

42.

Two days later Mr. Rodokonaki gave a great ball
for a hundred guests.

The diva, Mme. Schutz, dressed as a man, offered
a first performance of the victory march from *The
Prophet*, a new opera by Mr. Meyerbeer. A Parisian
magnetist magnetized an extraordinary medium.
The medium fulfilled all the wishes of the guests.

43.

The life of young Vitushishnikov was described
in one of the issues of *Readings*: "The Childhood of
One Hundred Famous Men," published at that time
by a bookshop specializing in life histories and

owned by Andrey Ivanov, in the building of the Cathedral of Peter and Paul on Nevsky Prospect: "The Duke of Wellington as a Child," "Fulton as a Child," "Count Kleinmichel as a Child," "The Wonder-Child." The last issue contained the life history and complete apotheosis of young Vitushishnikov. Subscribers in other cities paid for mailing costs by weight and according to postal fees. Requests were filled by the earliest departing mail.

His subsequent life is linked entirely with the history of closed military-educational institutions, the 5th Apsheron Regiment named after His Majesty the King of Prussia, and, finally, with the Exterior Department of the St. Petersburg Police (Inspector, 3rd District). But this already belongs to the time of the Chief of Police Blaramberg.

In 1880 the military historian S. N. Shubinsky, editor of *The Historical Courier*, visited the historical sentry box with its fully preserved memorial plaque. He was even able to find the guard. The spry old man sat at a table on which stood a wooden plate with slices of bread and some cheap vodka brewed with lime-tree buds.

"I remember him, sure I do, Your Excellency—a brave figure of a man. I looked up, and there he was. Came and took charge."

"But he was still young—a child?" asked the historian.

"No," said the old man. "What kind of child, a fine figure. Young, it was just his title. His rank in the Emperor's own service. Young . . . That's how he was listed."

"And the incident, do you remember that?" inquired the historian.

"The incident too," replied the old man. "I was there. I look—who's that coming? Rat-ta-tap, the Emperor. I hung this medal round my neck. Well, not this one. This one I got for that same incident. I hung another one. I came out, and I stand there waiting. All of a sudden, whoosh, and snow, smack in my face. I think—can it be the Emperor himself? And sure it was. 'What are you doing?' he says. 'Guarding you,' I say, 'Your Imperial Majesty.' And it was then that the incident happened. The infant got drowned."

"But they say that it wasn't quite so, they're disputing it," said the historian Shubinsky. "And the Emperor, do you remember the Emperor?"

"I remember," the veteran answered. "I saw him as clear as you. Wore a gray campaign tunic. And a military coat, wide open. The Emperor. . . . Sure. . . . Making the rounds. . . . The Turkish campaign was in his time. . . . "

Notes

Lieutenant Kijé

1. Potemkin, Grigory Alexandrovich (1739 - 1791). Favorite of Catherine II, the Great, and one of the most influential men at her court.

2. Brenna, Vincenzo, Italian architect, worked in Russia, 1780 - 1801. Cameron, Charles, Scotch architect, worked in Russia, 1779 - 1811.

3. Ivan the Fourth, the Terrible. Reigned 1533 - 1584. Sought to centralize and consolidate the Russian state, brutally suppressing the resistance of the hereditary nobility, the Boyars.

4. Grandmother Elizabeth—Empress of Russia. Reigned 1741 - 1761. Daughter of Peter the Great.

5. Allusion to the pretty villages Potemkin erected along the route Catherine the Great was to travel, moving them overnight to the next stopping place. The expression "Potemkin villages" has since become proverbial.

6. "The German imbecile." Reference to the erratic and mentally deficient Duke Karl-Ulrich of Holstein-Gottorp (born in 1728), half-German grandson of Peter the Great. Ascended the Russian throne in 1761 as Peter III, succeeding his aunt, the Empress Elizabeth.
    Assassinated, after a reign of six months, during the palace revolution of 1762, which placed on the throne

his wife, a minor German princess who came to be known as Catherine II, the Great (1729 - 1796), mother of Emperor Paul I (officially the son and heir of Peter III, but held to be of dubious paternity).

7. Suvorov, Alexander Vasilievich (1729 - 1800). Famed Russian military genius who led numerous successful campaigns under Catherine II.

8. Alexander Pavlovich, Emperor Paul's son and heir (born in 1777). The future Alexander I. Concurred in the conspiracy to depose Paul. Reigned 1801 - 1825.

Young Vitushishnikov

1. The term of military service under Nicholas I was 25 years.

2. Curb posts — low posts, about two feet high, set out along the sidewalk, probably to protect pedestrians from traffic (Russian *tumba*).

3. State Councillor, Privy Councillor, etc.—ranks in civilian government service.

4. Streets where the mutinous regiments marched during the Decembrist Uprising.

5. Reference to Friedrich Wilhelm IV, King of Prussia (reigned 1840 - 1861), who was pressed into making some concessions of a constitutional character during the revolution of 1848.

6. "At Enibazaar . . ." In 1828, during the Russo-Turkish war, Nicholas I, who accompanied the troops, caused the Russian army unnecessary losses by his inept orders. The Military Council induced him to withdraw from the field, citing the danger of encirclement by the enemy.

7. Concession, concessionaire (Rus. *otkup, otkupshchik*). A system under which the concessionaire leased from the government, which maintained a monopoly on the sale, and often production, of alcoholic beverages, the sole right to sell such beverages in a given area.

8. Grech, N.I. (1787 - 1867), writer, grammarian, co-publisher, with Bulgarin, of *The Northern Bee*.

9. Allusion to Peter the Great, who risked his life rescuing drowning sailors. (He contracted pneumonia, of which he died.)

10. Rode, Pierre (1774-1830), famous French violinist and composer, first violinist at the Russian court, 1803 - 1808.

11. King Otto I (1815 - 1867), son of Bavarian King Ludwig I. Placed on the Greek throne in 1832.

12. "an ancient utterance"—allusion to the Decembrist Uprising of 1825.

13. Railway tender—car attached to a locomotive, carrying coal, water, etc.

14. Ann Radcliffe (1764 - 1823), English writer of Gothic romances.

The Eridanos Library